WHAT

A second novel by author Susan Hausman that promises to keep you turning the pages late into the night as you root for the underdog…hoping her scheming husband's protective bubble finally bursts. Hausman's books continue to be hot and passionate with twists and turns and nail biting mystery. Don't miss the ending that is sure to leave you with your jaw dropping, wondering, "Can anyone ever really go home?"

—Dana M. Heiman
Vice President, Fund Development
for a Health and Wellness Foundation

Ms. Hausman has done it again! Just like in *Cable's Image* we meet characters who are very real, and bond with them upon introduction. There was an immediate connection with Stella; she could have been me or any of my girlfriends. I wanted to either counsel her or hug her at the turn of every page!

—Francine L. Jacoby
Senior Manager
A major Financial Institution

Split the Difference, the long awaited second novel by Susan Hausman, doesn't disappoint. Just like with her debut *Cable's Image*, Hausman has created a fast-paced and suspenseful storyline that engages the reader from the first page. Stella's journey forces the reader to ask how well we really know anyone, even the person with whom we share our bed.

—Stacy Mason, MA
Clinical Director
for a mental health agency

SPLIT THE DIFFERENCE

SUSAN HAUSMAN

SPLIT
THE
DIFFERENCE

TATE PUBLISHING
AND ENTERPRISES, LLC

Split the Difference
Copyright © 2014 by Susan Hausman. All rights reserved.

No part of this publication may be reproduced, stored in a retrieval system or transmitted in any way by any means, electronic, mechanical, photocopy, recording or otherwise without the prior permission of the author except as provided by USA copyright law.

None of the characters in this novel have any association whatsoever with a real person. This book was started long before a scandal about embezzlement broke in a community where I reside. That event was totally different from my plot. Any part of the story line that may seem the same is purely coincidence.

This novel is a work of fiction. Names, descriptions, entities, and incidents included in the story are products of the author's imagination. Any resemblance to actual persons, events, and entities is entirely coincidental.

The opinions expressed by the author are not necessarily those of Tate Publishing, LLC.

Published by Tate Publishing & Enterprises, LLC
127 E. Trade Center Terrace | Mustang, Oklahoma 73064 USA
1.888.361.9473 | www.tatepublishing.com

Tate Publishing is committed to excellence in the publishing industry. The company reflects the philosophy established by the founders, based on Psalm 68:11,
"The Lord gave the word and great was the company of those who published it."

Book design copyright © 2014 by Tate Publishing, LLC. All rights reserved.
Cover design by Joel Uber
Interior design by Caypeeline Casas

Published in the United States of America

ISBN: 978-1-63063-166-6
1. Fiction / Romance / General
2. Fiction / General
14.01.28

DEDICATION

To my ninety-eight-year-old mother, who in her beauty, wisdom, and great humor, has been an inspiration to our entire family.

ACKNOWLEDGMENTS

A special thanks to my husband, Larry, who continues to work feverishly for his author wife's success. Also, to my son-in-law, Peter, thank you for brilliantly designing my websites and for guiding me through my second novel.

Also by Susan Hausman
Cable's Image

CONTENTS

Dedication 7
Acknowledgments 9

Grooming Something Other Than a
Farm Animal 15
And Then Came Stuart... 24
Relatively Speaking... 33
The Smell of Money 43
The Passing of an Era 48
Deception, Force
It Runs in the Family.. 53
Whatever Stuart Wants, Stuart Gets, and
Little Stuart Wants… 55
A Model Example 59
Back to Monkey Business? 66
It's a rap 71
Filthy Money... 79
DNA: Do Not Annoy... 81
The Massage
Was Loud and Clear.. 88

The Ball Is In Your Court 92
Pass the Salt or Make A Pass? 97
Fashionation 100
Just Say Good Knight 105
The Secret Keeper 108
I'll Take Mine with a Lump of Sugar 113
The Audit 116
The Cleanup 121
Chemical Warfare 125
Plan B 129
The Worst Year of Her Life and the Breast 131
What a Dopamine! 135
Like Brother, Like Brother 137
Harry Houdini 139
Another Nasty Diagnosis 142
Up the Lazy River 146
The Book of Love 148
Food for Thought 154
Splitting Them Up 156
Eradicating the Pain from
Her Breast and Heart 161
The Discovery of Deception 163
All Squash Looks Alike or Is It Just Stuart? 167
Mirror, Mirror on the Wall 172
Triple Trouble 174
Collect Unemployment Plus Two Brothers 175
Old Memories; New Start 177
The Nail in the Coffin 179
Another Coke, Please 181
Malignancies of Her Life 183

The Disclosure 185
The Meal Ticket 188
Plan A, B, C... 191
A Mountain to Climb, or To Hide At A Beach? ... 194
When In Doubt…... 204
The Flight.. 210
The Performance... 212
God Bless America, Land of the Free:
God Bless Me!... 214
Let the Games Begin... 218
Roots 224
Headed to Jail, Not Aruba 232
Just the Beginning 234
A New Life.. 235
Embezzlement: You Are a Puzzle 240

GROOMING SOMETHING OTHER THAN A FARM ANIMAL

She pulled up to the dock in her boat and shut the ignition off. The house was just a few feet from the edge of the bay. It was early evening and the sun was just setting on a bright summer day. As she walked in, she heard the phone ringing. She threw her keys in the crystal bowl on the table in the foyer, pitched her baseball cap on the counter, and ran to get the phone on the third ring.

As she glanced out the kitchen window, she saw her neighbor, Jo Anne, in her striped bikini, taking in the last rays of sunlight on her patio and remembered the day she caught Stuart peering out of the sliders at her. Her cat, who they had cleverly named Cat-a-Comb, wrapped himself around her feet.

"Hello?" Her thoughts came back to the caller.

"Stelli?" Stuart always called her that. When he had first met her and asked her what her name was, she had told him it was Stella Yee. He had laughed in his charming way and asked permission to call her Stelli.

"What's up, Stuart," she said with the slightest annoyance in her voice. "Another late day at the office?"

"Honey, don't be like that," he whined. "I have to be on top of this client."

She laughed, hoping he didn't mean that literally.

With the economy in a major downslide, she should have been ecstatic that her husband was not only working but was also able to keep up with the payments on the steep mortgage on their summer home and the payments on their boat, as well as their McMansion on the Main Line of Philadelphia. She learned very quickly when they moved to the area that the Main Line was another name for the western suburbs of Philadelphia along Lancaster Avenue and the former Pennsylvania Railroad Main Line, extending from the city limits to traditionally Bryn Mawr and ultimately Paoli, Pennsylvania. Beginning in the nineteenth century, the Main Line became home to many sprawling country estates built by Philadelphia's wealthiest families. Today, it was a vibrant collection of exclusive and affluent towns including Gladwyne, the seventh richest zip code in the country.

Stuart and Stella loved the breathtaking scenery of rolling hills, open meadows, and winding roads adding to the glory of the area. They were proud to be a part of the affluent and fashionable region.

"I've already had dinner without you, Stuart." She tried not to sound sarcastic. "I took the boat out and stopped at Skifty's for a bite. I'll fix you a sandwich and leave it in the fridge for you." It was Thursday and he usually left the city for the drive to the shore to stay for a long weekend. Many times, he brought his work to the shore house. She didn't mind. At least he was around. But, lately, Stuart seemed to spend more time in the city.

Stuart cleared his throat. "Don't bother, hon. I won't be down until tomorrow, probably."

The living room was decorated in pale shades of color right out of a beach scene. The walls were seafoam blue and the sofa was pale peach. Shells from the beach adorned the cocktail table. The view from the living room was always Stelli's favorite. She loved lying on the sofa facing the water.

She slid off her sneaks without untying them and stretched out on the sofa, her long legs hitting the arm of the sofa at one end and her long blond hair hanging down over the arm of the sofa beneath her head. Cat-a-Comb jumped up and laid down near her bare feet. She was so tired from being in the boat most of the day. Her stop at her favorite waterside restaurant had renewed her slightly. She didn't mind eating alone. It was peaceful and the place was alive with other customers, some who she knew from the shore area. The sun had been strong and beat down on her, even though she had put on a baseball cap and her sunscreen.

In no time, she had drifted away to a cloud floating in the sky, but it was made of barbed wire.

When she was born in 1983, her momma and daddy had brought her home from the hospital to the farm, where they lived in rural Minnesota. The town was called Thief Runnery and little did she know that the name would be indicative of her life to follow.

The townspeople of Thief Runnery were an honest bunch; the worst crime some of them committed was to gossip. The name did not go with the people who lived there. Perhaps, the town ran no more than a mile wide and a mile long. It had a pool hall, a gas station, a grocery, a beauty parlor, a liquor store, and a country café, where all the old and retired farmers would sit in a corner and play cards and drink strong coffee all day. They gossiped more than the women did.

The café was decorated with country knickknacks. Teacups hung from hooks on the walls and they alternated with plastic apples, which always seemed to Stella to be growing right out of the walls. She had been in the café one day when a mother and her baby were sitting at a table near the wall. The baby had reached out from his highchair and grabbed an apple right off the wall. He had put it in his mouth to eat when his mother grabbed it away, laughing hard. She, too, had giggled at the sight.

When summer would arrive, Stella would beg her parents to take her to the county fair, the Demo Derby, and even the Harvest Bazaar. She was always bored and always nagging her Momma. She had no siblings to play with and always felt a nagging sense of loneliness and isolation.

"When are we gonna go, Momma?" This was her summer chant. At least when school was in session, she would hang out with her friends and they could entertain each other. They could sit for hours and braid each other's hair. They even tried on their mommas' lipstick and performed plays for each other. Stella always had chores to do, but in the summer her daddy made her go out early in the morning and feed the chickens and hop on the plow with him to head out to the fields.

She was so bored.

Stella shifted position and continued to dream about her early life.

For Stella's high school graduation, her momma had promised her a manicure at the beauty parlor in town. She had gotten very tall and very beautiful and had long blonde hair that was often braided down her back and it would bounce up and down as she ran.

She dreamed of moving away from Thief Runnery and exploring the world.

Stella switched her position on the sofa so her head was facing into the back of it. She curled up and continued dreaming. Cat-a-Comb woke at the movement and inched his way closer to her belly, where he could feel every breath in and out.

Cat-a-Comb moved from her feet and stretched across her thighs. She didn't stir. Her sleep had carried her away to another time.

It had been one of those summer days when everything and everybody dripped with perspiration. Even the mosquitoes were hot! But the beauty parlor had a huge fan on the ceiling and it whirled around while the manicurist did her nails.

She remembered the day clearly.

The lady sitting next to her had started a conversation.

She had turned to face her, with her body in Stella's direction, but her hands still being held straight ahead so that the manicurist would not miss a stroke of red polish.

"How old are you, honey?"

"I'm seventeen. I just finished high school and Momma gave me this treat as a graduation gift." She pointed to the Pretty in Pink polish for her own nails.

The lady smiled and said that she was visiting an old aunt in town and that was how she came to be in Thief Runnery.

"I'm really from New York, but my Aunt Becky —do you know her?— she has lived here all her life and she's getting up there in years and I just wanted to come see her."

"Your Aunt Becky?" Stella's manicurist patted her hand to stay still. "Is it Becky Halcomer? She's the nicest lady! I sometimes go over to her house and play with her cat."

"That's my aunt!" she seemed to say proudly.

She went on. "Do you have any idea how gorgeous you are?" Her newly polished fingers sliced through the air from Stella's head to her toes.

The manicurist was done with Stella and she swiveled her chair to face this lady, who was dressed like a mannequin in a very fancy shop window.

"By the way, my name is Anne Kohlner and I just happen to work for a modeling agency. Would you consider coming to New York?"

Momma had not been happy. The modeling scout had come over to meet Stella's parents and tried her best to woo them with promises of Stella's success. Anne handed her business card with the name of the modeling agency on it and wrote on the back of the card her home address in New York where Stella could stay with other girls she was mentoring. After much convincing, she promised that Stella would call twice a week and be given the freedom to come and visit frequently. "Why, you can even come to New York for a visit! Wouldn't that be so much fun?" Anne smiled persuasively.

"This was the worse possible present I could ever have thought to give you. You cannot go to New York. How will we take care of this farm without you?"

And that was all Stella needed to hear. She could not bear the thought of staying on the farm for the rest of her life. This was her opportunity and she was not about to miss out on it. She pleaded and cajoled and her parents were just too tired to argue with her.

The suitcase was packed as lightly as possible. Anne had told her that she would add to her collection of clothes when she began modeling. Stella took one last look at her room, dragged the suitcase down the stairs, and kissed her parents goodbye. Her mom and dad were stoic people and they just stared ahead as she walked out the door. She headed to the car that Anne had sent to pick her up and take her to the airport. As they drove away, she kept waving to her folks who had walked out and were standing on the porch. She forced a big smile and glanced around at the farm that was once her refuge. The palm of her hand left a print on the foggy window.

She headed for New York and the promise of big things to come.

Beauty Management. That was the name of the ultra trendy agency. It was very modern in appearance and Anne had promised her that she could get her started with a career. She put up several young girls in her own huge four-bedroom condo and mothered and nurtured them all and dealt with their ups and downs in a very kind way. She had told Stella how cutthroat the business could be, but she would watch over her carefully. Anne treated the girls with respect.

Stella had never seen such a beautiful apartment. It was modern with dots of Asian motif scattered about. Mirrors glistened and called to their vanity. The girls were always primping, even in the hallway.

There were some editorial campaigns and some runway work, both in the American and global market, and Stella traveled and traveled and always came home to Anne. She felt an obligation to do her best and to be devoted to Anne. She felt as if her boring life had been injected with excitement by her.

She would call her mother and father every Sunday, but there was always this icy response from them each time she tried to tell them about her career. Her dad had always been direct and cold, like the Minnesota winters, and never minced words with her. He rarely spoke, but when he did, it was to criticize her or to keep her reeled in.

Momma would sigh and Daddy would just listen on the extension, grunting every so often. She felt guilty, but she also felt pleasure and a sense of wonder at all the possibilities in her new life.

AND THEN CAME STUART

There had been negotiations on a particular project that Stella was hired to do. She was entering into a higher priced contract and lawyers had become involved.

Stuart Crane was walking down the hall of the law offices of Borders, Crane, and Yelds when Stella was heading towards her lawyer's office. Their eyes had met; Stuart put out his hand and instead of a professional handshake, he had patted her hand. "I'm Stuart. I'm one of the partners here. Welcome aboard." After what seemed like an eternity, he had gently dropped her hand, which tingled at his touch. "What about coffee after your meeting? We'll properly welcome you as a new client to our firm." His smile was arresting and the rest was history.

"Have you been sleeping here the whole night?" Stuart was shaking her awake.

"Stuart? I thought you weren't coming home tonight." She shook herself awake, sitting up with a startled look, and Cat-a-Comb seemed to imitate her. "What time is it?"

Stuart sat in the chair across from her. "It's the morning, Stelli. What's going on with you?"

She was starved. She couldn't believe she had slept on that sofa since walking in the door at eight last night! Something was wrong with her. Had she been in a deep sleep for all those hours?

Stuart walked into the kitchen as she was fixing breakfast. The pots hung above the granite counter top and Stuart glanced up to get a look at his image in the frying pan. *You would think he was the model*, Stella thought to herself, amused by his vain action. "I got here fairly early this morning. There wasn't any traffic coming down." He took his usual stool at the kitchen counter. "Wanna go out on the boat after we eat?"

Stella scraped the last of the scrambled eggs off the plate and put it in front of Stuart. He grabbed a fork and started poking at the eggs, changing his mind and instead grabbing the crispy slice of bacon and crunching it in his mouth.

"Stuart, I was on the boat all day yesterday. I think I'll pass." She put a bite of egg in her mouth and reached for the knife to butter her bagel.

There was a moment of silence as Stuart swallowed his food.

"You were so anxious for me to come down the shore and now you don't even want to bother with the boat. Why do I even bother coming down and, more importantly, why do I even bother paying for the stupid boat?" He crossed his fork with his knife, making an X on the plate with his silverware. Stuart was always so neat and so proper.

"Don't be unreasonable, Stuart. I've been feeling tired lately. I just feel like puttering in the garden. You go, and we'll have dinner together later. Should I make reservations at your favorite restaurant?" She got up to clear the dishes, placing them in the double sink. The kitchen featured beautiful white cabinets with silver pulls and stainless steel appliances stood at attention. They had redone both their home kitchen and their shore kitchen around the same time, using the same contractors for each. The men had been perfectly willing to travel to Philly for a hefty fee. Two contracts in one fell swoop! They must have thought they died and went to heaven!!

She heard the motor of the boat and watched Stuart from the sliders. He was muscular and handsome and everything that a girl could possibly ask for in a man. He wore a T-shirt that showed off his muscles and chocolate brown bermuda shorts. His black sunglasses made him look like a movie star. The boat shoes were naturally worn without socks so he could look as cool as possible. Stella should have felt lucky. She didn't know what was missing, but she just didn't feel right.

The casino had a pier where the boat owners would dock and go in and spend some of their money at the slots or tables. Stuart was very happy to be among the players, and he was glad that Stelli hadn't wanted to take a boat ride with him. Any time he could get away from her, he would relish the idea of racing through the waters to the casino. She was such a backward farm girl and would rather have been at a zoo or farm than be surrounded by all the glitz and glamour that had practically made him swoon with delight. He had felt that way when he first met Stelli. She seemed so glamorous and so beautiful. She would make a great trophy wife. But, she had remained naïve and always felt awkward making small talk at the various parties they had attended. She made an entrance, having learned how by being a beautiful model, but once all eyes were on her, they couldn't get her lips to say a word. She seemed shy and awkward around others and often had to just pretend she was performing a modeling job so she could ease her way through the crowd.

The sparkling chandeliers and the bustling of the dealers and cocktail waitresses and people looking for a quick win like him enticed him like no woman could. It was almost better than sex, titillating and exciting and demanding. Once in a while, Stella would agree to go with him on a Saturday night, but he would leave her at one of the penny slot machines and go find a table where he could show his skills at poker or blackjack.

Out in the garden, Stella kneeled to feel the dirt beneath her fingers. She had grown up hating the farm, but she had loved the beautiful garden that her mom had cultivated. The various aromas that wafted from the colorful flowers always made her feel alive. Even the worms beneath her fingers would remind her of trying to wiggle free. She had always prayed that one day she would shake herself free of the farm.

Her great-grandparents had immigrated to this country and settled in Minnesota to farm the land. They had raised a large family, one of them being Stella's father who would continue the family tradition. He had married Stella's mother, and she was more than willing to be a farmer's wife. Neither of them had aspirations beyond the soil. Her great-grandmother had created a tradition of soap making and Stella's mom occasionally continued the custom when she found the time. Oh, but she could also bake a mean lemon meringue pie! Stella smiled at the thought, turning the soil. She couldn't believe how slender she could stay even with her mother's delicious cooking and baking. Often, there would be get-togethers with the other neighbors and they would hop in their truck with Stella sitting on the flatbed, holding her mom's potluck contribution as if it were gold, her long hair flapping in the wind as Poppa drove fast.

But, most of all, she loved her garden.

Now, Stella's own garden was alive with the most beautiful plants and looked like a Monet painting, awash in lavenders and golds and bright oranges and pinks. There were pink coneflowers and blue lavenders, white Shasta daisies, and black-eyed Susans. She whirled the dirt around in her fingers and tried to think about how lucky she was to be there.

Stuart had wined and dined her before they married and he was attentive and romantic and caring. His promise to provide her with everything she ever wanted was an enticement beyond the world of modeling. She may have walked the fashion runways, but she would now walk side by side with Stuart.

Across the table at a fine restaurant one evening, he had leaned over to her conspiratorially and asked her to marry him. He brought a huge diamond ring out of its box and flashed it in front of her wide eyes. Why, it was practically the size of a hen's egg! And, it was then, at that moment that everything was right with the world and she had said yes.

When dessert came and the shock of the proposal had still been with her, Stuart had at last said what he had been thinking the whole evening. "The only request I have in this marriage is that you give up your modeling career."

Even though they had a pool in their backyard, they drove to the beach on occasional Saturdays, leaving Cat-a-Comb behind, meowing his anger at them as they walked out the door to the car. They were several blocks from the beach and had to use one of their cars to drive there. Each time they would go, they shoved two beach chairs into the back of the car and took a cooler filled with lunch and beers.

They chose an area of the beach where there weren't too many people and settled down in the sand. Stella slipped off her cover-up and flip flops and adjusted her bikini. They each read, hardly speaking the entire afternoon, and ate independently of each other when they each felt hungry. Stella was mesmerized by the ocean and looked up from her pages frequently to watch the waves hit the shore. She would never tire of gazing at the ocean or even appreciating the water that filled their swimming pools. A couple walked along side the ocean's edge hand-in-hand and Stella thought that she and Stuart seemed like two strangers who just happened to be sharing a piece of the beach together. He had not even glanced at her when she took off her gauzy iced blue top that matched her suit. Stella was lithe and willowy and had worked out feverishly. Why did he practically look through her as if looking on the other side for something else? She watched him fall asleep in his chair with his head to the side, his shirtless chest beginning to redden from the sun, and found herself thinking about how she had given up her career for him. She had started to resent it early in their marriage after looking for things to keep herself busy with and finding that nothing was rewarding. One more lunch with the ladies, one more visit to the gym, one more reservation at a restaurant, and she would scream. She had talked to Stuart about opening a boutique. Certainly, he would agree to that. It wasn't modeling, after all. Stella had even thought of a name for her store. She would call it Fashionation.

But, when she had presented the idea to him, he had said no. He made tons of money and he had frequent social engagements for her to attend at his beck and call and if she got busy running her own shop, then she couldn't be available to him. He gave her everything she could possibly want. No, it was out of the question.

She had acquiesced. Stella didn't feel like putting up a fight. She wanted to make this marriage work and she would be there for him when he needed her. She had sacrificed herself by growing up on a farm and never protesting; she had learned well. She wouldn't protest now. With every phone call home, her parents had asked the same question: "Why did you bother leaving home if you couldn't continue your career?"

Anne had called her one morning while Stella was talking to her housekeeper. She tucked her hair behind her ear and picked up on the second ring.

"What are you up to these days, Stella?" There was no wondering about who was calling. Anne had the sweetest and most caring voice.

"Anne! I have missed you. I don't know what I'm busy with and I can't come up with any good excuse, but I have been trying to be the good wife to Stuart." She giggled uncomfortably.

Anne sighed. "My darling girl, you must come back to work before you get too old for modeling. Why, Stella, you must be all of twenty five by now!"

They both laughed. "A tad older. But just a tad!"

The suggestion had sounded very tempting, but Stella knew Stuart would be unhappy with any decision she made to go back into modeling. She had promised him that one thing when he had proposed and she just couldn't go back on her word. He hadn't liked the idea of her opening a fashion boutique and he certainly wouldn't like the idea of her going back to modeling.

She twisted her wedding band around on her finger. "Please keep in touch with me, Anne, and keep me posted about how the modeling business is going for you and your ingénues." She sadly hung up, feeling as if she were in mourning for the life she had wanted so badly to pursue and had so disappointedly failed at having. Was she destined to live vicariously through Anne every time she called Stella?

The tide was rising within a few feet of their chairs as she came back to reality. She looked over to see Stuart still asleep. He was snoring softly in rhythm to the waves lolling ashore. She got up and collected the trash and slipped into her flipflops.

She jolted Stuart awake. "It's time to go back."

The weekend flew and although they kept busy with their usual activities, Stella was feeling depressed. Her sad mood had started before Stuart arrived, but it escalated with him there. Before he drove off early Monday morning, she woke from her sleep to wish him a good week. A few more weeks and summer would end at the shore. She would be back to a different routine in Philadelphia. Maybe she was just ready for it to end.

RELATIVELY SPEAKING

When Cotton Masterson eyed Stuart as he passed her desk, he turned and gestured with his head for her to follow him into his office. She gathered a file from her desk so she would look like she was conducting business. Seesawing on very high heels, she slowly worked her way to his office.

"Close the door, Cotton. You got here earlier than I did. Did you miss your Stuart over the weekend?" He snickered.

She wore a short black skirt and a ruffled white blouse and no stockings. She knew it looked better if she wore hose. That would be office-appropriate, but she wanted to be prepared for Stuart when he arrived. The office was pretty quiet in the early hours of the morning and Cotton had rushed to get to work so she could have some time with him before things got crazy. Every Monday would be the same routine. Stuart would drive back from the shore and she would be ready for him. Once the senior partner arrived, it was all business.

He ran his hands through her long red hair. "You are so beautiful, Cotton. I can understand why your mother nicknamed you that. You are as soft as cotton." He felt himself getting hard.

When Steven Crane left his office building, he was carrying a box filled with mementoes of his years of service at Platto's Physical Therapy. He had been happy there until one of his clients had told his boss he had overstepped his massage and she accused him of attempting to rape her. There had been no amount of explaining to get out of it, since the customer was always right as far as his boss was concerned. His twin brother, Stuart, had always had the brains, but he had brawn mixed in, making him the twin to contend with. It had taken him far with his female clients and his bookings were always scheduled one after the other. Occasionally, a client would get annoyed if he let his fingers manipulate the wrong area. The oils in his palms would act as a conductor between the masseur and the lady. He would start with their scalp and rub it gently until the client was completely relaxed. He'd move to their neck and shoulders, barely brushing his fingers against their breasts. Steven would move up and down on the arms of the woman he was massaging and run his hands in circles around her belly. Up and down the legs, always careful that his hands didn't caress her private area. He would pull gently at her fingers, one at a time, and then move to her toes and massage them until the client would practically be putty in his hands.

He had never had one complaint, let alone an accusation of rape. Steven would never stoop so low. Sure, the very act of massage would sometimes excite him. The room was warm, the music soft, and upon occasion he would get hard. But rape? Massage was more than an indulgence. It was a therapy that promoted good sleep, reduced aches and pains, and boosted a person's immune system. In most cases, if he were successful at his job, the person would feel like they had just finished a run. Their blood pressure would lower, not rise as if they had just had sex. It wasn't meant to enhance the masseur's physical performance.

Sure, Steven thought, *it lowered his anxiety level. But rape? She's crazy!* He threw the box into the backseat of his car just as the police car pulled up.

"Mr. Crane?" The cop towered over him. He was blond, blue-eyed, and broad-shouldered. He looked like a Nazi to Steven. His partner stood next to him as if they were mirror images like him and his brother.

"Let's go inside and have a talk. Then we'll need to head to the precinct. We have a few questions for you."

After Stella had her manicure, she leaned into her manicurist, Phe No, and although the young woman could hardly speak English, Stella thought she could share her feelings with her. She had been feeling so alone and this one day every two weeks Phe No would offer her the "therapy session" she needed. Mostly, she would nod her head as if she understood everything Stella said, but today was different. As she buffed

Stella's nails, she listened intently, occasionally clicking her tongue in sympathy. Stella's manicures had led to all kinds of revelations: first, when she met Anne, who would change her life. Now, with this appointment, she was exposing herself not to a new world as a model, but as a young woman on a path to her collapsing world.

"Phe No," Stella said, blowing carefully on her wet nails. "I think my husband is having an affair."

The manicurist didn't do her usual nodding gesture. Instead, she got up from her chair and came around to hug Stella. "You be careful of naughty man. You get AIDS or something." She turned to the manicurist next to her and said something in Vietnamese. The young woman put up a hand to her mouth in shock.

Those words haunted Stella daily. She was so afraid to approach Stuart. He was, after all, so busy with his legal practice and she didn't want to rock the boat. She was still that farm girl at heart and women listened to their men as though it were another century or perhaps even another planet. Her mom obeyed her dad with every one of his requests and in spite of his demands, they were always loving with each other. She would look at him as if he were a king, sitting upon a throne, instead of a bale of hay. His overalls were like a tuxedo to her mom and he could do no wrong. One night when Stella was hiding behind the banister, she watched her parents doing a little dance to soft music in the living room. They had moved the rocking chair away and had rolled up the rug and her father hooked his fingers into the straps of his overalls and did a little jig before sweeping her into his arms. Stella thought it was so cute and she was happy to see his soft side. She had wished for a man like her papa at that very moment.

When she arrived home from the shore after Labor Day, her neighbors were happy to see her. Stella had made friends with the neighbors when she first started walking around the neighborhood. The homes were large with immaculately groomed lawns and she would rarely see anyone unless they were either getting into their fancy cars or running or walking on the hillside like she frequently did. Strollers were being pushed by stay-at-home moms, dogs were being walked, and on weekends, bikes were everywhere. But, she had been delighted to run into her next-door neighbors one day when she walked past their driveway. They had waved and the wife had come down the long driveway to speak to her.

Stuart had been very annoyed when Stella had suggested that they come for dinner one evening. "He's black, Stelli, and she's white. What's the matter with you?" he questioned in a mocking tone. "How will it look if I associate with them?" She couldn't even respond to his hideous statement and felt tears rising to the surface. She ran off to get a tissue and didn't come to dinner that night. He had not understood her acceptance of this biracial couple. Her acceptance! Wasn't that the idea, to be accepting of all people until they would prove it wasn't deserved? He had been very annoyed and when he came to bed that night, he slammed the bedroom door closed and threw his clothing on the floor in a bunch, pulling back the covers dramatically. When he slid in bed beside her, he turned over and moved to the edge.

She hadn't cared one bit. So what about the neighbors? Who did he think he was? They could afford the house next door to them just like Stella and Stuart could. The husband was a doctor and the wife was a hospital administrator. She hated that he had such an ugly prejudice. But later on, Stella would make excuses for Stuart and would suggest going out with them without him. After all, he was a busy man with a very tight schedule.

In the morning, they were back to their normal behavior. Stuart raced to the bathroom to get an early start and, with the bathroom door ajar, Stella watched from the bed as he stared at himself in the mirror. He was a handsome man, with dark waves of hair, one curl adrift on his forehead, chocolate brown eyes, and ears flat against the sides of his face. She had to admit that they were perfect ears. They didn't always hear her very well, but they leaned against his face, not flapping out like they were ready to put him in flight. She always seemed to pay attention to a person's ears for some reason and she had thought from the beginning that Stuart's face was perfectly symmetrical. She had been in a world of beauty and it appealed to her in a way that others might not even care about. She wasn't shallow, but the indefectibility of a person's face was like looking at a beautiful piece of art in a museum.

He seemed to know how handsome he was; every time he passed by a mirror in the house, Stuart would smile back as he walked past, showing his beautiful white teeth, like rows of tiny monuments, recording his perfection.

"C'mon, Steven." Stuart tugged at his brother's sleeve. "Mom said we had to stay outside and keep out of her way today." The teens were always underfoot and their mom wanted them out of the house. Their neighbor, who was a carpenter, was coming to build bookshelves for their Mom and she had scooted them out the front door. Stuart was angry. He would never forgive his father for leaving them when they were so young. He and Steven hardly remembered him. A piece of him was missing and he was sure his absent father made him feel that way. Sure, they had the basics in life with a roof over their head, food on the table, and bare necessities. But, he would always want more and more. Didn't he deserve a better life? They were young, but their mother was already drilling the word *college* into their brains. They would have to save every penny from their paper route and she was always stressing hard work. Sometimes, he felt like the male version of Cinderella. Tears burned his eyes. Mom was always busy with the men in her life since their father had left her, but she still tried to instill hard work in them.

Steven had loyally followed his twin brother down the street and on to the main avenue where the neighborhood stores were located. "Where are we going, Stuart?" He stopped in his tracks to question his brother, the larger of the two. Although they were born just a minute apart, Stuart had always acted like the much older brother, pushing Steven around.

"Can you be quiet for one minute? I'm going into the drug store to get some comic books!" He shoved Steven on the back in the direction of the store's magazine rack.

"Where'd you get the money from?"

"You are beginning to annoy me a lot."

"We already spent the money Mom gave us on gum and candy and she isn't going to be happy if she finds out we're stealing comic books," he said, as his eyes diverted from the scores of choices.

Stuart glared at him. "Mom isn't going to know, now, is she, Steven? If you say one word, I'm gonna give you two black eyes."

"Where'd you get the money?"

"You asked me that already!"

"I'm more scared of Mom than I am of you. Answer me."

Stuart reached for a comic book and flipped through its pages. "I took the money from her wallet. She'll never miss it. I'll pay for the damn thing!"

They lived on a shady street, lined with maple trees and cookie-cutter houses attached to each other like Siamese twins, with more front lawns than back lawns. As they walked back from their little excursion, Stuart shoved his comic book into his brother's hand. The sprinkler on their neighbor's front lawn was on, spraying an invitation for someone to jump right in. Although, most of the houses had fences around their small neatly manicured lawns, the gate swung open here as if to say, *Come in, play with me.*

"Mom's gonna kill you if you get wet!" Steven stood rigidly outside the gate.

"Come on in, Steven, the water's warm." He laughed, attempting to torment him. "Forget about Mom. Let's have some fun before cranky old Mrs. Chapson chases us away." He curled his arms toward himself for Steven to jump in.

It was still September and it felt hot to Stella. Stuart was always in a rush for her to pack up the summerhouse and get back to their primary residence. She understood his dislike for the long drive to the shore every week, but it was so peaceful by the bay.

She folded a lacy pair of underpants into the drawer. She didn't need sexy underwear very much since Stuart hardly made advances anymore. If she initiated sex, he would jump at the chance, but he satisfied himself quickly, never caring how she felt. He would roll off of her and turn on his side only to leave her wanting. The satin sheets felt cool against her needy body and acted like a mini–air conditioner to bring her temperature down. There might as well have been a vat of ice in the bed because Stuart made it feel like a freezer.

Where had things gone wrong? Where were the days when he brought her flowers and candy? She remembered the day he had left a gift box on the kitchen table where she could find it when she came in to make breakfast for herself. When she tore open the wrapping paper, she had found a box of gumballs and in among the crayon-colored candy were two diamond earring studs. She had been so excited and when he had come home that evening she had been happy to show him how thrilled she was.

There hadn't been a gift in recent years. He barely remembered her birthday and surely didn't remember their anniversary. But then, he was so busy with his law firm and he worked long hours. How could she expect him to take time to search for just the right present?

Or was he giving the gifts he used to give her to a new woman?

THE SMELL OF MONEY

The aroma from the baking bread wafted through the house. Stella loved getting her hands into the mixture of yeast, water, flour, a little sugar and salt, and some oil. She kneaded it, making it feel warm and happy, ready for the baking pans. She punched the dough down, divided it into three parts, and sprayed the pans. The same emotions she was feeling seemed to be poured into making her mixture. First, she was warm and happy to be baking and then when Stuart slipped into her consciousness, she felt a great sense of relief in getting rid of the anger by pounding the dough, imagining his face on each loaf. Her mom used to bake all the time and it was these memories that kept her grounded. Stella always watched her roll out the dough and form little scoops for cookies or bigger sections for bread. She baked frequently and when she rolled out the dough, she pounded it with a vengeance. Maybe she too was taking out her frustrations in the kitchen.

While the bread baked, she slipped into her bikini and readied herself for a morning swim in their pool.

The weather was changing to fall, but she swam her laps, grabbed a towel, and dashed back into the house. She wouldn't be able to swim much longer. It would have to wait until it was close to summer again.

She slid the loaves out of the oven and left them to cool on the granite counter. Stella headed for the shower.

Stuart made sure he was in the office before Cotton was even getting out of bed to get ready to come to work. He had taken a day off here and there without telling Stelli or anyone in the office where he was going and he had driven down the expressway to the shore. He would sit and gamble and spend the entire day at the tables. The money was thrown on the table, the cards were dealt, and invariably, Stuart would lose. Just a little more cash, a few more dollars, and he was sure to win a hand. He rubbed the green felt and tapped his fingers on the poker table. Once, he had been dealt two aces and excitedly pulled a third ace and another pair. The winnings had been big. But the following week, he had traveled to the casino again, only to lose what he had won the week before. The money was flowing like the smooth, uninterrupted highway he had driven. But it mostly flowed into the dealer's hands and emptied out of his wallet. It was a good thing that they had comped him for a meal and drinks or he would have gone without. The comps meant any item of food on the menu was free. Even the booze was free. He kept just enough aside to get home. No one would be the wiser as to his whereabouts.

Cotton's office was between his office and that of the senior partner. He opened her door and closed it behind him. Her desk was cluttered with files and work to be done. She was assistant to the three partners, but she assisted Stuart the most where it counted. He opened her desk drawer, glancing at the door to make certain it stayed shut as if it were to pop open at any moment. It was still too early for her to be strolling in. He was imagining things. The sweat formed on his brow like rows of coins. The petty cash was in a box and it was conveniently unlocked. He wasn't about to bring that to her attention. This would make it much easier for him to grab a few dollars here and there. The firm kept easily accessible petty cash on hand for all kinds of incidentals and wasn't his gambling a current circumstance that made it necessary to lift a few hundred bucks now and then? He'd figure out a way to get cash for his habits. Quickly, he reached in, took the money, made sure another hundred dollar bill was folded on top, and closed the box. Then he walked out and closed Cotton's office door, sighing with relief that no one had entered while he was rummaging through her file drawers.

He laughed to himself as he walked back to his own office. He was really stealing from himself and his partners. But this was penny ante stuff and he needed a way to support his love of gambling and his love of a beautiful lifestyle. He remembered when he first saw Stelli. She was gorgeous and he just had to have her. What was life without surrounding himself with beautiful objects of desire? His partners were strictly buttoned-up, conservative men with boring lives. Even their wives were plain and boring. Granted, he had tried to bed Karen, the wife of his younger partner, Joseph, but she had said she would never mention the incident and that he must never even look at her cross-eyed again. She acted appalled, but Stuart knew the real truth. She was probably delighted with his flirtation, a pass she couldn't have had since she met her husband. He was sure it was probably the only proposition she ever received. If it hadn't been for nerdy Joseph, she'd still be unmarried and unbedded! She was nothing much to look at, and after all, Stuart was handsome, charming, and complimentary. He had surely made her day. The turndown was her mistake and her loss. Although he had eyed her hungrily, her commitment to his younger partner was admirable. *But maybe a little foolish*. He would have taken her places he was pretty sure she had never been before and that virgin-like act would have melted into thin air. *Well*, he thought to himself, *there were greener and more gorgeous pastures where she came from*.

He poured himself vodka from his office bar and sat down to think about where he could obtain some big money. The ice clinked in the glass as ideas formed in his head.

The phone rang and Stella put down her magazine. She had stared at the models and yearned for those days. She was still so young, but when she looked at their faces, fresh as the ink on the pages, she realized just how young the girls were. She had been a teenager when she started her career and it had been cut short when Stuart came on the scene. But she longed to get back to work—if not modeling, then something in fashion.

THE PASSING OF AN ERA

The phone rang for the fourth time and she grabbed it. It wasn't her neighbor who might have gotten a whiff of her baked goodies. The houses were far enough apart, but good aromas travel far!

The name was unrecognizable on the caller ID. *Was it one of those annoying marketing research companies?*

Annoyed, she barked, "Who is this?"

"I'm trying to reach Stella Crane. Is this Stella?" the caller quickly questioned.

"I'm speaking. Who is this?" Stella removed her earring, while she nestled the phone in the crook of her neck.

The caller's breathing was coming through the phone like a soft breeze.

"This is Vanessa. I'm Anne's daughter. I got your phone number from her cell phone. I've been calling all of her contacts." Her breathing got heavier as if a storm were about to brew. "She passed away two days ago. The funeral is in New York at her estate. She is being buried under her favorite tree. Since you knew my Mom so well, you must know how esoteric she really was!"

"How do you like your dinner, Stuart?" Stella put her napkin on the table and pushed her chair out to go to the kitchen for dessert. This was one of the few times Stuart actually made it home for dinner at the right time.

The tray held one of Stella's specialties, a banana chocolate chip cake. She had taken up baking as a way to work out her frustrations. She cut a slice and placed it on the fine china dessert plate, outlined in a circle of gold. She wore a circle of gold on her wedding finger and it was eating her up alive.

"Anne died, Stuart." Tears welled up in her eyes, blurring her vision. She gave up on cutting herself a slice of cake. "I need to go to New York tomorrow for the funeral. Will you come with me?" She picked at the crumbs that had fallen on the side of the dessert tray and mindlessly swiped them onto his plate.

Stuart looked up from his food long enough to glance at her and say, "I have way too much to do, Stelli. You can handle it by yourself. You certainly knew her better than I did."

The funeral was arranged in Anne's garden, with folding chairs lined up facing her coffin. It was just like Anne to want beauty in death, as she did in life. Most of her models were there, at least the ones who could fly from their assignments and get to the funeral on time. There were agents, photographers, magazine editors, and all kinds of people from the fashion industry, and, of course, all of her family members, already shredding tissues wet with tears even before the priest began to speak. Many stood behind the last row of the chairs already occupied. A cool breeze had started to blow and the leaves were circling the coffin, draping Anne in autumn's farewell embrace.

At the reception, Stella mingled with the guests. She knew some of them from her stint as a model; however, there were so many new faces.

"Cassandra! We haven't talked in ages! How are you? What are you doing these days? Are you still modeling?" She rattled off the questions like shots from a rifle.

"Stella! So good to see you!" Cassandra flipped her hair away from her blue eyes. "It's been too long. I'm out of the modeling business. At age 26, they sent me to pasture! I'm married with two children and I'm opening a boutique in Manhattan on the first of the month. I want to get rolling in time for a good Christmas season! You must come to the opening."

The Ferrari California was a midfront, eight-cylinder car that boasted a sporty feel and maximum driving pleasure, all qualities he liked in his women. It had a classic sculpted chassis and the car salesman had been chomping at the bit when Stuart started his inquiry.

The commission would help feed this man's family for a very long time. He practically fell all over Stuart in gratitude. Stuart had driven over to the agency in his Infiniti and when he pulled up at a red light, he was sandwiched between a Mercedes and a BMW. It just reinforced his desire to drive something even more impressive. Let everyone pull up at a red light when he's driving a Ferrari. They will drool!

"I'll take the car in red. Order it for me," Stuart demanded like a man who was used to getting what he wanted.

He was on such a high when he returned to the office. He couldn't get the smile off of his face. He had wanted everything in life since he was a little kid and he was well on his way to obtaining it all. *Hmmm*, he thought to himself, *maybe I ought to learn how to fly a plane.*

The papers were strewn out before him. He had entered his office, closed the door, and reached for Mr. Sult's file. Mr. Sult was his oldest client, with no family willing to manage his estate. He was an old neighbor of Stuart's family and when he had learned that Stuart was practicing law, he had called one day and asked him to handle his affairs. There would be a fee, of course, but how easy would it be to take a little here and there that the old man would never notice? He could pay for his Ferrari, maybe pay off his mortgages, buy a plane, buy a—well, he could figure out a way to buy anything he wanted without losing a moment's sleep.

He could just start a fake company and incorporate it. After all, he was a lawyer, wasn't he? He could figure out a way to get money out of that rich old client of his without him ever knowing it. That could put money in his pocket with no problem and no one the wiser.

DECEPTION, FORCE IT RUNS IN THE FAMILY

When Steven saw the two men, badges flashing in the sunlight like sparkling mica, he felt his stomach flip. He walked them up to his front door and they went straight to his sofa without an invitation to sit down. They were there to question him on a client's allegations of rape, and he started to perspire and open and close his fists in nervousness. It was a motion he had perfected ever since he was a little boy. If he were nervous, he would use his opened and closed fists as a way to release the stress he felt. Like kneading clay, he could create a new form and erase his life even if it were just for a moment. He would capture the air in his closed fist and slowly open it so the air could escape. He, too, felt like he was escaping. When he would try to fall asleep, with his brother, Stuart, in the bed next to him, mocking him, belittling him, Steven would open his fist and use each finger to silently sing "Doe a Deer." His thumb reaching out was Doe; his pointer and middle finger, a deer; his ring finger and pinkie, a female; his thumb on the other hand, a deer; until he would finally settle down and drift into sleep.

Thinking about his current dilemma scared him. Would he have to move away, change his name, change his life, run from what was likely to turn very ugly? Damn, he had just massaged her inner thighs. He had rubbed down his clients, using his fists for something besides capturing air. He would pretend he was molding his clay and making the form take shape. He couldn't help it if she took that as molestation or even rape. How would he prove himself? It was her word against his. Any DNA would not show up as rape. He'd just have to set up shop far, far away. They didn't have any proof to send him to jail. Maybe his brother, Stuart, would have some ideas. After all, he was a lawyer. Maybe he could get him to give his input over the phone (if he could ever get a hold of him) and offer him advice on a defense. Stuart wasn't licensed in his state, but he would get in touch with him and ask him if he should stay or go. He'd know the ramifications. He hadn't talked to him in a long time, but Stuart would surely be there for him. Wouldn't he?

After a few minutes of standard questions, they took him out and slid him into their cruiser.

WHATEVER STUART WANTS, STUART GETS, AND LITTLE STUART WANTS...

She put her overnight bag down and placed the key in the lock. Stella felt so sad and weighed down. Her carry-on felt so much heavier than it really was, and the thoughts running around in her head were making her feel like she had weights strapped to her brain. It was horrible to say her last goodbyes to Anne, a woman who had given her so much. Stella wouldn't be in this beautiful house or at the shore or in a boat or anywhere but the family farm, if it hadn't been for Anne. Yes, Stuart had earned a handsome living, but he had not been the one to discover her. It had been Anne. She had been her mentor and friend and if Stella had any backbone at all, she would have called her to get her input. Anne would have pushed her to open a store or, for that matter, jumpstart her career again. She wasn't that old to return to the modeling world.

Her image looked back at her in the hall mirror and she pulled at her face to look for those telltale fine lines. Gosh, she wasn't even thirty. Why was she feeling so old? Maybe, this would be the right time to call Cassandra and see what it took to follow her dreams. They hadn't had much time to talk alone.

Stuart would just have to accept it. He was always on time handing her allowance as if she were his child instead of his wife and she had been smart enough to save a portion of it in her own personal account. Each week he'd hand her money and she would make a point of taking some of it to the bank. She had earned a lot of money modeling and that was hers to keep, but she added more to it in the hopes that one day she would be independent again. Stuart had been her wizard, conjuring up a magic life for the two of them. She was getting fed up with his magic tricks.

"How was Anne's funeral?" Stuart said, with a laugh. He was standing in front of the sofa ready to sit and relax.

Stella faced him, angry. "How could a funeral be, Stuart? You should have been with me."

"Oh, honey. I bought us a Ferrari. I'm getting it Saturday. Maybe we could take it for a spin before it goes into the garage for the winter." He grabbed the day's newspaper off the end table, still preferring to hold the news in his hands and not read it on the computer. He plopped onto the sofa.

Stella glared. "With a summer house and a boat, do you really need to spend that kind of money now on one of the most expensive cars on the road?"

"Need?" Stuart raised his voice. "Need? We don't need anything. I want it. And what Stuart wants, Stuart gets! Why are you being so small-minded? You slide right back into your hick beginnings!" He opened the paper with such force that the page tore right down the middle.

There was no dealing with him when he got on his high horse with her. How dare he insult her! She had made a name for herself and had given up everything to be his little wife. She was more determined than ever to pick Cassandra's brain and find out what steps to take to open her own boutique. More and more frequently, she found herself turning away from him in a huff, disgusted with what they had become as a couple.

"Cotton, give me a hand in my office. Now, Cotton." Stuart was in the mood for some loving and she was convenient. If anyone in the office overheard his comment—his double entendre—they couldn't question whether she was about to take notes or take him. Her blue sweater set was the color of robins' eggs. It hugged her body and highlighted her curves. She wore a chocolate brown skirt that just skimmed her knees and her legs were bare, even though winter was fast approaching.

"Let's get some more petty cash in your drawer. There, we talked business! And now close my door. We have some other things on the agenda!" Stuart slowly lifted her chocolate brown skirt, hungry for her sweetness.

Up until now, he had dodged the infidelity bullet. Stelli thought he had integrity and that he had been loyal to her all along. After all, the shore house, the boat, the big house on the Main Line, and now the Ferrari – who else would they be for? His perks were Stelli's perks except for any action he took on the side. And, Cotton was all action.

Cotton pulled down her skirt and straightened her sweater set. She slipped on her high heels and quickly glanced in her compact mirror to make sure her lipstick wasn't smeared.

"Stuart, I'll check on that petty cash right now. Don't forget to zip up your fly."

Clive Borders was Stuart's senior partner. When Cotton came into his office asking for more petty cash, he was a little puzzled.

"Cotton, I gave you money two weeks ago. I thought it was needed monthly. Are you keeping an eye on the staff and their needs?

Are you locking the drawer? You are in charge of petty cash and I don't want you to come running every time the money is low and the month isn't even up," Clive said, in an annoyed tone. "If they are using this money for the vending machines, I'm pretty pissed about it." He shooed her away from his desk as if he were dismissing a lowly servant, without giving Cotton a chance to respond.

A MODEL EXAMPLE

It was an early snow. Late November came far too quickly and Stella faced the cold, sitting in her backyard by the pool and stretched out on one of the chaise lounges that had never been put away after early fall. Stuart had been too busy; he was always too busy. And she was formulating her plan for her new store. She put her tongue out and let a snowflake make its landing in her mouth. The meteorologists had predicted several inches of snow, but compared to her childhood winters in Minnesota, this weather was a piece of cake. She could not figure out what made the locals run to the store for milk and bread as if they would be stuck in forever. The plows were great about getting rid of the snow and it was easy to get out, usually the next day after a big storm. You didn't even need a flag on your antenna to be seen when you drove around a corner.

She wrapped the cashmere blanket around her. She was wearing her parka and boots, but she was chilled to the bone. She gazed at the pool, covered for the winter, and wished she could be swimming in it. Her thoughts began to swim around in her head. How to start this business?

"The first thing you need to do is create a business plan. Make it convincing, thorough, and detailed, so you can get a business loan." Cassandra made it sound like Stella was buying a cake at the local bakery instead of selling herself and her idea.

Cassandra rattled off all the points to cover for the plan as if she were dictating to a secretary who took shorthand.

"First, your vision statement. Then your economic assessment and basic business concept. You should list feasibility and specifics as well as your focus and concept. Write a comprehensive business plan! Think of it as a road map to help you embark on this journey. And, don't forget to add in about capable management," she said with the enthusiasm of a hurricane about to hit town.

Stella wrote as fast as she could. She would dot the i's and cross the t's later. "Keep it simple, girlfriend." She laughed. "These three-piece-suit-wearing bankers may be boring, but they get bored by others too!"

"Oh," Cassandra continued breathlessly, "a marketing plan! Write an in depth marketing plan! Crucial! You want this to be profitable! What will you name it? Where will you get your inventory? I'll help you with that. I have contacts all over New York and you have to choose your price points for your merchandise. You're gonna have to invest lots of time and money into this.

Don't leave advertising out of your plan. Let's see. What else? You'll also need to host an opening event with giveaways and food, or coupons for premium items."

"How about a fashion show? That's right up your alley? "

"Did you get it all? You better invite me to your opening, too! "Cassandra spoke without inhaling.

He wrote the first check to R. C. Brown, specialists in home health care. *This was going to be easy*, Stuart thought, as he filled in the amount for $2,520 to cover Mr. Sult's full-time aide and the various costs to manage his home. The old man wouldn't ever spend a nickel to pay for help. He chose to meander around his huge mansion with a walker and no help. He had food delivered to his front door weekly and that was his only extravagance. Well, couldn't Stuart pretend that he had a home health care aide? He had opened an account in the counterfeit name of R. C. Brown and it would be easy for him to create on his computer falsified invoices from a fake company and put them in the fraudulent account. His receipts would have the made-up name of Mr. Sult's aide and all the services she performed for him. He could even double-dip both accounts to pay for Mr. Sult's weekly prepared foods. Oh, there were going to be plenty of ways to take the old coot's money. He was harmless and simple. Sure, he knew how to make tons of money in his day, but he was 98 years old and didn't give a damn about his money anymore. He had given Stuart full reign over his kingdom and Stuart deserved all that he could get out of it for his hard work. With today's medical advances, who knew how long Sult would live? This charade could go on indefinitely if the old man continued the way he was going.

He could start looting the old man's assets. Knowing Mr. Sult the way he did, the guy would probably leave everything to an animal shelter. He was just wacky enough to do that. Didn't Stuart have more entitlement to his money than to be paid just a lousy executor's fee? Maybe Stuart could set up an offshore bank account somewhere. He was a smart lawyer and he had genuine talent. Stuart could orchestrate this fraud. He could start out small and end up stealing on a massive scale. The 98-year-old had stocks that Stuart could put his hands on. He could even file fake multimillion dollar claims on behalf of many of his clients. There was no end to the path to all the money he could ever want.

He hit the enter key on the computer.

"Hello?" Steven yelled into the phone. "Is that you, Stuart?"

"Who is this?" Stuart had been deep in thought when the phone rang. He was thoroughly annoyed that someone would call him in the middle of a brilliant thought.

He heard the laugh and immediately recognized it as belonging to his brother. He had the same sound, the same tone, and the same power to his voice.

"Not now, Steven," he said, scratching his nose. "I'm way too busy to shoot the shit with you about your little massage business. I've got a law practice to run here." He shuffled the papers on his desk and stuck a pencil in the sharpener.

Whir, whir, whir.

Steven wasn't going to take no for an answer and kept talking. "I have a business problem here and since you're such a big city lawyer, maybe you can give your brother some advice."

He tapped the pencil point on his desk. "Let it wait, Steven. Call me when I'm not busy, which is never, haha," he stated sarcastically.

Click.

She was bone-tired. Stella had worked for hours on her business plan and her brain felt like it was filled with cells, but of a different kind. Jail cells, holding her ideas locked up in prison. It had to be perfect. She was going to do this on her own. She wasn't sure yet if Stuart had to get financially involved, but she would fight him to the finish line for her dream. She adjusted her bra strap, sliding it back onto her shoulder, and thought about the amount of money she would have to invest without begging Stuart for help.

When the Ferrari pulled into the driveway, Stella was not inclined to start dancing around Stuart's moods. It was probably best that she blurt out the truth about the boutique idea and just get it over with, but she shouldn't have to feel sick to her stomach with the thought of facing her husband. Why couldn't he be easy to talk things over with? His charm and wit had carried him a long way, but this marriage was starting to feel too heavy.

"How was your day?" she nervously asked.

"Oh, just dandy. This law crap is for the birds. And whom am I working this hard for? My beautiful wife, who gets to live this life!" He dramatically drew his hand in a large circle, pointing to their belongings. He jabbed his finger toward the unseen pool. Angrily, he stuck his fork into the pot of meatballs and shoved a whole one into his mouth.

"Whew. They're too hot, Stelli! Can't you do anything right?"

She led him to the dining room table. It was so infrequent that he was home at dinnertime and she would take advantage of this time face-to-face, two opposing teams discussing the strategy.

"I've been thinking, Stuart." She spooned the gravy over the meatballs. Pouring the vodka into a glass to help soften his foul mood, she put down the decanter and went to the desk in the den to get the papers she had been working on. "Here. Take a look at this, honey. You won't have to worry so much about paying our enormous bills if I'm willing to help."

She seated herself across from him and watched him take a sip of his drink. He gingerly bit into another meatball, half afraid that it would burn his mouth again. "I'm not interested, Stelli. I've read enough documents today to last me a lifetime. Let it rest." He pushed the papers across the table toward her, purposely stretching his arm and practically lifting himself out of his seat, so that the papers would reach their destination with drama. He made his point loud and clear.

"Dammit, Stuart!" she screamed, surprising even herself. "I want this for myself and I'm doing it with or without your approval!" Her fork slammed down on the plate. I'm not a five-year-old who you can lead around at your will." She continued to raise her voice. "You asked me to give up my career for you, for your stupid ego, so I could hang on your every word and be at your beck and call for all of your moronic clients! Well, I'm afraid that ship has sailed. I'm doing this, Stuart, like it or not." She moved away from the table. "And that stupid Ferrari! You were supposed to keep it in the garage during the winter months. Who needs it? You can't drive it fast on these suburban roads. It's just for show. I would rather show *myself* what I can accomplish."

Oh, he liked it all right. She was turning him on. He had never seen her so angry since he met her. The hell with the meatballs. There was a hotter dinner waiting for him. He got up and went over to her.

"Baby, settle down. We'll work this out. Let's forget about dinner for now. Rub my tense shoulders. I'll rub your feet and we'll massage away this discussion for now. It's been a long day." He put his arms under hers and lifted her up to face him. He could turn her into a character in a romance novel. He scooped her up and headed for the bedroom, with her trying hard to wiggle away from him.

BACK TO MONKEY BUSINESS?

The necklace felt like cold, smooth satin against her face. There were tiny diamonds spread across the chain like sprinkles on the top of an ice cream cone just clinging on to the top. She rubbed it across her cheek and spun around and lifted her tresses.

"Hook it for me, will you, Stuart?" Cotton wiggled her fanny at him and giggled.

"You shouldn't put it on today. Someone's liable to notice when you walk out of here that you have something new around your neck. Just come in nonchalantly with it on next week, and if anyone asks where you got it, just say your boyfriend is getting very serious with you and gave it to you over the weekend." Stuart turned her around to face him and smoothed over her red hair. "Honey, this has to be our little secret, remember?"

Cotton made a childlike boo-boo face and whined, "This little secret can't be kept forever, Stuart! How long do we have to keep it quiet?"

"Forget about that," Stuart said nervously. "I want you to do me a favor, sweetie." He ran his fingers lightly across her cheek. "I want you to put some expenses in for me. I had dinner with a client the other night, but I forgot the receipt, so just put in for $159.65. Oh, and I'm taking this client to Aruba for four days. Gotta wine and dine him to death. I'll give you a list of the expenses and you can handle the numbers." He thought to himself, *It should be easy to compromise her integrity. And Clive, as senior partner, wouldn't be missing small chunks of money anytime soon.* When Stuart became a partner, he had to make a capital contribution to the firm, but that was long ago, and now he had to take back what was rightfully his and then some.

The firm was successful, though not successful enough for Stuart's taste. Clive took the bigger percentage as senior partner, having started the company. Stuart had been at the right place at the right time and Clive wanted him to handle the litigations, deal-making, and even some real estate law. He felt they would work well together, as they both wanted to fulfill the same goals. Stuart was younger and Clive had felt that he was very capable. Revenues were good, but nothing was ever good enough for Stuart. Why should Clive get the bigger piece of the pie? He worked as hard as Clive, maybe even harder. It was time for him to get a bigger bite. They kept lawyer headcounts at a steady pace and continued to grow. Clive had even made one of the top attorneys in the firm a junior partner, right along with Stuart. How dare he! Corporate activity was at a high and no one would ever miss the money. Stuart was going to take what he deserved. The other partner was catching up to Stuart in the salary department and that pissed him off, too. He was a lot worthier than these doofuses.

Lightening lit up the dark sky and the thunder made Clive jump. Bolts of icy metal sliced through the dark day making it look like night. He adjusted his bow tie and swiveled his chair around to face the huge window in his office. It was still winter, fighting to become spring, and the weather was so erratic lately, like it couldn't decide what personality it wanted. Did it want to be freezing and snowy? Did it want to throw lightning bolts to the earth? Warm one day, cold the next—it was temperamental like his employees could be. True, he was the senior partner, the managing partner, a role he was growing tired of filling. All these management functions were getting tiresome. He had supervised personnel and the firm was growing, making his hours at work fill up as if someone with very large hands was pouring a million details onto his plate and he could not keep up. If the springs on the clock sprung and Clive couldn't tell time, he would still have to fill up the time with endless details of work. The hands on the clock may stop, but his hands were in piles of items that had to get done. It was an endless expenditure of his valuable time. He wasn't feeling any younger, either. In the beginning, when Stuart first came on board, Clive was steadily at the helm, steering the cash flow management and accounting on a huge wave of success.

He attempted to motivate his partner and manage the associates. Lately, he had felt that Stuart should take on some of these responsibilities. When did Clive become too busy to practice law? The combination of senior partner and lawyer was becoming a mix of bananas and soup. They just didn't work too well together. And the newest partner was just that, new. He had asked Stuart to come in for an early meeting that morning.

"What's up, Clive?" Stuart seemed very nervous.

Clive shuffled some papers on his desk as Stuart sat down in the burgundy, leather-studded chair facing him. "I think this managing partner deal is wearing me out. It feels like both roles are beginning to suffer. I can't be the lawyer I intended to be and manage every business detail too." He absentmindedly turned the framed family picture around to face Stuart.

They had ended up huddling in Clive's office for much longer than they had intended, discussing their goals and objectives and Clive passing the ball to Stuart in certain areas where he could alleviate his load.

"I'm inclined to let you give me a hand with at least the money management. What's your take on that idea?" Clive stood up to indicate the meeting was over.

In small law firms, there is a common reluctance to get involved in management for the very reason Clive was passing some of the responsibilities to Stuart. Normally, a partner would balk at the idea of more on his plate, but Stuart walked out of Clive's office with a huge smile and thoughts of how much easier it would be to manipulate the funds. He would have the support and encouragement of the senior partner and that would make his job a lot easier. Stuart had a vision; after all, he had a stake in this firm, too. But, that vision would be a little shortsighted and not go much further than his own bank account. He'd have more prestige, respect, and authority. Who would possibly question him about the finances? He'd be careful to take a monthly management fee even though it hadn't been offered. Maybe he'd list one of the other lawyers as the recipient of that fee. Who would know? He wouldn't let this extra duty cut into his billable hours either. And Cotton would have to spend more time in his office helping to guide him with his goals. Oh, he had lots of goals, for sure. *Won't be able to make it home as often, anymore.* He chuckled to himself.

IT'S A RAP

Steven was getting very pissed off at his brother. He had tried to communicate with him on several occasions and had gotten nowhere. Now, he was hung out to dry all alone. He had always felt like a broken piece of Stuart's mirror image. Something was always missing. He just couldn't figure out how to please his brother as hard as he tried. His twin seemed to always be searching for something and even though their father had left the family, his twin had always been right under his nose. They could have roared up together like the head of the horse and the tail of the horse. But Stuart was always at the reins, pulling away from his twin.

    He knocked his head on the roof of the car. "Dammit!" He rubbed his scalp. The radio was blasting with rap music and the two cops were bobbing to the tempo. Steven, attempting to think about anything but his troubles, pounded his hands on his knees in beat to the music and moved his long legs up and down to the rhythm. They got to their destination about twenty minutes later and pulled into a parking space right in front of the round police building. On the way over for the twenty-minute ride, he let off steam and wrapped his mind around the rap music they were all listening to. What a weird choice of music for the cops! But, they, too, were letting off steam. He didn't want to focus on the problem at hand until he was face to face with the detectives inside.

"Have a seat, Mr. Crane." The detective waved him into the metal chair opposite him. Plastic cups and an institutional-looking water pitcher sat on a long table behind him. A trashcan sat in the corner. There was a huge map on the wall with pins punched into different locations. The room was small and poorly lit with dark gray walls. It looked just like all the other police interrogation rooms he had seen on detective shows that he watched on TV. At that moment, Steven wished he could be anywhere in the world but where he was.

"You can have counsel present, but that might take a while. Why don't we go over some details while we wait?" He lifted his eyebrows at Steven as if to show understanding.

"I've been trying to get a hold of my brother. When the cops came by for me, I tried a few times without any luck. He's a lawyer. He doesn't practice in this state, but he could advise me," Steven chattered aimlessly.

The detective ignored him. "Now, let's see. According to this document, you have at least fifty clients for your massage business. Is that correct?" He was poised to write any answer Steven would give him.

"Have you ever had any complaint from any of your clients before this time?"

Steven shifted his long legs and crossed them opposite of how he had been sitting. "Uh, they never complained while it was feeling good." He tried to get the detective to laugh with him, but he would have none of it.

The inquisitor rolled his chair more tightly under his desk and got as close to Steven without pulling some science fiction move to slice his chair through his desk and jam it up against Steven's knees.

"There's no need for jokes, Mr. Crane. This is a very serious situation. You are being accused of rape. Your client is in the other room right now being interrogated by another one of our detectives. I suggest you get your story straight." He opened up the desk drawer and pulled out a letter opener and sliced open a large envelope sitting on top of a pile of papers.

He slammed the drawer shut. The simple movement made Steven jump. "Truth is, they never complained, whether they liked the massage or not. One or two might get a little fidgety when I had to massage the inside of their thighs, but they didn't exactly move away. And this client, sir, never once complained while I was in the massage room. I was always very appropriate with her. I'd leave the room when she got undressed and always told her to be under the sheet when I came in so none of her lady parts would show. It was a solid hour of her practically snoring while I rubbed away her aches and pains. And she tipped really well!"

His legs were getting stiff sitting in the chair and he quickly uncrossed them and stretched out. He kicked the desk by accident and quickly sat up straight.

"No, sir. I never touched her inappropriately, let alone rape her. No, that four-letter word is not in my vocabulary." He folded his hands in his lap, not knowing what to do with himself.

The detective's pencil slid down to the next question. "Answer the rest of these and you can go. But make yourself available in case we need to call you in again," he said, as he got up and sat on the edge of his desk.

Steven was sick of this game. His client was acting like this was some television show and they were just actors playing their parts. Well, this wasn't a part he wanted to play. He was no rapist and if she was just looking for attention, this was a hell of a way to get it. They'd test his DNA and see for certain that he'd never violated her. She wasn't going to corner him. He'd think about leaving town and never coming back to this city, a town staged to pounce on its decent citizens. They should blame the bureaucracy for attacking Steven, not for Steven attacking this woman, who clearly was looking for the wrong kind of attention. If only he could get a hold of his brother and make him listen.

"Hit me." Stuart tapped his fingers nervously next to his dealt cards. He had to reach twenty-one without busting. The ace stared back at him. It was paired with a three, which was the face-up card for all of the players to see. He could turn that ace into a one or eleven to help his hand add up to twenty-one. He looked up at the "eye in the sky," the video camera located above the table making a recording of the entire game. It was used to help resolve disputes or identify dealer mistakes, but its main function was to protect the casino against dealers who steal chips or players who cheat. Stuart wished he could get around this casino advantage, but he owed them money and he didn't want to add another layer of trouble to his laundry list of money problems.

There were seven people sitting at the semicircular table. They each placed their bets in the betting box at each position in play. One of the players shoved a cigar in his mouth and chewed wildly on it. This drove Stuart crazy. At one point he elbowed the man just to get him to stop this disgusting act and the man had gone right on chewing on the tip. It made Stuart's stomach feel nauseous.

The single card flew out of the dealer's hand, across the table, fluttering until it reached its destination.

The house advantage with a double deck of cards was 0.46 percent and Stuart had played cards at these tables long enough to know where he stood on the win-lose scale. He used his great memory, strategic thinking, and observational skills to create a superior position. He had even read *The Shuffle Tracker's Cookbook* by Arnold Snyder. It mathematically analyzed the player's edge.

Some casinos were providing electronic consoles to play different table games. He preferred to watch the real people sweat.

He slowly flicked back the corner of the dealt card. It was always about the thrill and the drama, the heart racing, the belief that the gambler would win. And, if he wouldn't take this hand, surely he would take the next.

It was a seven!

He reeled in the pot, each dollar a fish swimming in shark-filled waters.

He clearly had better than average luck. Maybe tomorrow he would play poker.

It was a perfect day. The sun was bright, hanging in the sky like a big, yellow birthday balloon, and Stella felt rejuvenated. Maybe she needed a play day to rest her brain. She had worked so hard on her business plan and although that had been challenging enough, Stuart was even more so lately. He was moody, angry, and defensive. She couldn't quite put her finger on what was wrong, but he was not himself. She had a fleeting and unsettling thought that perhaps he had been to the doctor and had been told something that unnerved him. She would put aside any annoyances and ask him first chance she got.

Why not a drive down to the shore on such a beautiful day? She could be alone with her thoughts and once she was at the slot machines, she could forget everything. Gambling was fun and therapeutic and she always forgot her troubles when she walked into a casino. She looked upon it as entertainment and was always in control of her money. Stella had worked way too hard to throw it away. Yes, they were comfortable and could afford to use the money in a fun way. She always thought of it as spending money she would use for a lovely dinner out, a movie, a show, or some fun activity that fell into their entertainment budget. Luckily, Stuart earned good money and they could live the good life. And now that she was considering opening her own boutique, there would be more of it, for sure. The shore house had not been checked on all winter; perhaps Stella could do that as well.

The casino always thrilled her. Throngs of people were laughing and having a good time. The restaurants were filled and the players sat eagerly at their slot machines anxiously awaiting that big win that probably would never come. The tables had a sprinkling of poker-faced players waiting for their next card to drop to the green felt and change their lives. If only most of them realized it was just entertainment and it wouldn't pay their monthly rent, there would be no need for Gamblers Anonymous.

Oh, crap, Stella thought to herself, as she strolled past a section devoted to poker and blackjack tables. *"What is Stuart doing here when he said he was at work?"*

That was her fastest stay at the casino.

"Mom!" Stella tapped her fingernails on the table. She switched the cell phone to her other ear and opened the refrigerator to grab a yogurt.

"Why, honey, it isn't even a Sunday! How come you are calling early?"

"I just had to vent, Mom. I decided to open a clothing boutique and Stuart is being a hard-ass about it—please excuse my language! He wants me at home to be at his beck and call and I'm sick of it. I gave up my career for him and I'm not willing to give up my whole life! Her voice went up an octave. "I hate to say it, but

I'm starting to regret ever leaving the farm. Life is too complicated here!"

Her Mom tried to interject. "But—"

"No buts about it. I took a personal day just to run away from myself and I drove to the shore for a little gambling expedition and to check on the house and…" She knew she was rambling.

"It's okay, dear. Maybe you should come home to rest for a little while. You know what they say about absence." Stella could hear her Mom laugh nervously.

"I saw him at the poker table, Mom. He was supposed to be at work. He never told me he was taking a day off to go to the casino," Stella snapped.

Her mother paused. "Well, you didn't tell him either."

FILTHY MONEY

Another workday. There was definitely an easier way. He could sit at the blackjack or poker table just as easily as he could sit here. Damn, he wished he didn't have a pile of folders sitting in front of him. Stuart had to at least look busy and try to do his job. Otherwise, how was he to get his hands on this money? At times he felt like he was stealing from himself, but his partner took the largest chunk and he would even out the playing field.

He felt chilled and reached for the phone to buzz Cotton into his office.

"Could you get somebody in here to check the heater?" He attempted to sound sarcastic. "It's freaking freezing in here! What's the company, anyway? I'll call them myself... But of course, you could make me feel a whole lot warmer." His caustic tone dissolved.

When Cotton finally left his office, his mind started racing. This could work very well. He practically reached around to pat himself on his own shoulder for being so clever. Stuart looked at the past bills from the heating company and took the white out to erase the figures charged. He entered a bigger number on each invoice and went to the copier himself. If he played around with the bills enough, it would be easy to adjust the charges. Maybe he could pull this off with other vendors who did work for the firm. He'd just have to look into the cleaning services. This would be a cakewalk. He swung his chair around to face the computer and forgot that he had opened the file drawer. "Damn it." He bent down to rub his knee and when he lifted his head, he banged it on the desk. Was this a sign from God? *No, I don't think so*, Stuart thought to himself, not knowing what to rub first. *God wants me to be happy.*

DNA: DO NOT ANNOY

They didn't have much. In the early morning, the two brothers would take turns pitching the morning paper to all their neighbors. Stuart got great pleasure out of racing his twin between the houses and trying to throw the newspaper farther and faster to the front doors than Steven could. It infuriated Stuart that he had to share the money with a brother just because he was his twin. Steven was everywhere Stuart turned. Their mom, Margaret, insisted on it. Whatever Stuart wanted to do, Steven had to do. She had even tried to dress them alike. She was overprotective and wanted them to not only be identical in looks but also exactly the same in behavior. Well, that was where he drew the line. No way. As a little toddler, he had rolled around on the bedroom floor as she tried to put him in an outfit that matched Steven's. Eventually, she gave up. As they got a little bit older, their mother had tried very hard to allow them to act as two separate individuals, just as the doctor had done when they were born. Hadn't he pulled them out separately from their mother's womb? Mom always seemed conflicted. In the earlier years, they were forced to do all identical things; as they became teens, she wanted them to be more individual.

They might have the same DNA, but he was going to try to be as different from Steven as possible. His brother annoyed him constantly and he'd never have the brains Stuart had.

In their biology class one year, the students had been taught the basic tenet of human biology that identical twins come from the same fertilized egg and thus share identical genetic profiles. *Well, they might look alike*, Stuart thought, *But that's where the line was drawn*. He knew that although he and his twin share very similar genes, they were not identical in many ways. Two people who hailed from the same embryo could still differ. He had checked it out at the local library.

As they got older, the differences became more and more clear. While Steven ended up going to the same college as Stuart (Mom wouldn't hear of them separating at two different schools), he clearly leaned toward physical interests. Stuart was more cerebral and clever. Each time Steven was in Stuart's presence, he would complain feverishly if his brother lit a cigarette or even ate a hamburger. One night they were hanging out with some friends at a local bar frequented by the college kids, when Stuart had ordered a cheeseburger.

"You know, bro, tobacco and the kinds of food you eat accumulate in your body over a lifetime and you are throwing away a lot of years to your life," he said, smiling knowingly.

Stuart had asked his buddy to slide out of the booth so he could stand for a minute. He slugged his brother and said, "If you ever lecture me again, I will personally break your neck. Eat your damned tofu and shut up."

He had known that behavioral traits like fearfulness that Steven showed and confidence that Stuart showed would affect both of their lives and certainly Stuart's for the better.

They may have shared the same womb at the same time and even the same gender, but that's about all they shared. They had established their own individual likes and dislikes at an early age. Steven wore those stupid overalls and always looked like a little farmer. He dragged around a stuffed horse, tying a leash around its neck, and pulling it behind him wherever they went. It made Stuart look stupid. He was cool and didn't need toys to make him happy. He had often wished for another brother who he could turn to for support instead of having to always act like the big brother. Why was their Mom so obsessive about them being together all the time?

As teens, Steven would finally put the dumb horse away and he would join any sport he could. He actually became good at all athletics and Stuart was not going to let his brother outshine him. He decided to concentrate on his schoolwork and sharpen his academic skills so he could go to a good academic university. Steven's body might be fast, but Stuart's mind was faster.

As they grew up, their differences became greater. Their fingerprints weren't even the same.

Their school buddies had always called them the mirror twins because they looked so identical, but actually mirror twinning is comparatively rare in humans. They might have dark, wavy hair and blue eyes and the same strong nose; they were the same height and about the same weight. But when they smiled, Steven's mouth turned up slightly in the corner and Stuart's was a perfect slice across his face.

When Steven caught a cold, Stuart would get sick a week after. When the allergist diagnosed Steven with childhood asthma, sure enough Stuart received the same report. Well, he was sick of having the same illnesses as his brother.

His mom had chuckled at the idea of separating the boys and putting them in different rooms. "This isn't the Taj Mahal," she had said, laughing. "We don't have a spare room for you to sleep in, Stuart. You'll just have to be happy sleeping in the twin bed next to your brother and remember to use your own glass when you brush your teeth."

Margaret had been obsessive about the boys ever since they were babies. She wasn't about to lose the sons she had fought so hard to keep. Her husband had walked out. There were just too many mouths to feed.

Seth got out of his car and yanked the nozzle out of the gas pump. He watched as a man with his teenaged son gestured to the pump next to his own car. He was teaching his boy how to pump gas.

Seth's mind wandered. He remembered fondly how his adoptive father had bought him an old jalopy when he turned sixteen. He too had shown Seth how to pump his first gallon of gas for his very own car. His adoptive parents were wonderful people, but he couldn't help but wonder why he was given away. When he had turned twelve, they had told him he was adopted. There was no back story, just that they had adopted him and loved him as their own flesh and blood. He remembered feeling nauseous when they explained about his adoption. He could never shake his curiosity or that feeling in the pit of his stomach about why his real parents had chosen to put him up for adoption. Was he so horrible as a baby that they couldn't love him? He thought he had turned out pretty well.

He squeezed the handle to get the last drop of gas into his tank. The man at the next tank hugged his son and they got into their car. Seth had wanted to start searching for his birth parents but it would have hurt his adoptive parents too much. He was a grown man. Wasn't it time to try?

Sure, he had lost his job as a teacher. Teaching positions were so hard to find in his small town. But, he was a good person. He would relocate if he had to and make his home in Anywhere, USA. Once settled, he would start his search.

The nozzle clicked off, shutting off that memory for the moment. He placed it back in the pump, paid for his gas, and drove away.

She loved shopping. She loved fashion. After all, she had been a model—not just a hand model, but a full body model, posing with beautiful clothes that were the latest fashions. This was her passion. This idea was going to work. She had been so frustrated when she last spoke to her mom. Perhaps she did miss the solitude and peacefulness of the farm. She had certainly come a long way. She would try to make this idea work.

Stella spent hours on her business plan. She would buy the clothing and accessories from wholesalers and set the prices. The doors would open to customers eager to snap up her latest selections. They would tell all their friends and the boutique would be a huge success. She was already an insider to fashion trends, even though she had retired from the business. Stella still read every fashion magazine that was on the market. Creativity played a huge role and she could give expert advice to her customers.

The boutique would be chic and have personalized service. It would have a cozy ambience and high quality clothes.

It was time to get the ball rolling. Stella would need to go to the bank and acquire a business loan. She had plenty of collateral to put up. The shop would open in a fancy mall with high customer traffic.

This would be Stella's passage to peace. If she stayed out of Stuart's way and restarted her career, albeit in a different form, she would work long hours and they could meet at the end of their business day and have so much to talk about. He would have a renewed respect for her. Freedom, independence, and real financial security on her own terms would make for a fulfilled wife and a satisfied husband.

The long mirror was framed in antique brass and stood alone in a corner of the bedroom. Stella strolled over to it. *Yes. There are flaws.* She pulled at the corner of her eyes. She was close to thirty. In model lingo, that was old. She stood alone like the mirror and when she looked at her image she said, *There will be no flaws in this boutique. Everything will be perfect.*

THE MASSAGE WAS LOUD AND CLEAR

One lousy client and I'm practically banned from doing my job, Steven thought, as he walked to his car after another attempt at getting a job as a masseur. He had tried to apply for the few jobs that had been listed in the paper, but with the economy the way it was, little was offered. He thought about the interview for the massage position.

The owner of the spa had invited him in to her back office. She was in a black leotard, with a miniskirt, black leggings, and ballet flats. She must have been confused with the type of business she was in. Did she think she was a dancer or a spa owner?

"Steven," she had said. "It's very casual around here. No mister or miss to address our employees. Hope you don't mind the informalities." And then she had taken his resume and paused long enough to read it quickly. "Your last name is Crane?" she questioned. "Aren't you the guy who was accused of rape recently?" She snapped her head up to stare at him.

That girl had not only gone to the police with her story of rape, but to the papers!

The interview felt similar to the police interrogation.

"We can't use you here. For that matter, it's my opinion that you won't get a job anywhere in this town. Your so-called client has accused you of rape and everyone must know about it." She squirmed nervously in her chair. "You may be innocent until proven guilty, but until the matter is cleared up, our customers might feel very uncomfortable around you. This is not good for business. Sorry." Her chair screeched against the bare floor as she pushed away from the desk.

He slid into the car. "Damn it!" He hit the steering wheel with his open hand. *She's ruining me. The only physical contact I ever had with her was a proper massage. Why did she come back a second and third time if I was being inappropriate?*

The detective sat on the edge of his desk facing the accuser.

"This is the third time you've been in my office, Miss, and I'm still not clear on this accusation. Were you or were you not raped by Steven Crane?"

She sat up straight and placed her open palms on the desk, brushing the side of his hand. She tittered, "So sorry, officer."

He was annoyed with this girl. Did she have the nerve to flirt with him in the interrogation room?

He flipped through the pages of the report. This guy, Steven Crane, was accused of raping his client, but wasn't it easy for an unstable woman to mistake a massage for rape? The physical contact, especially by a man, could feel like a violation if the customer drifted off and dreamed of his hands and body being all over her. Physical contact could be misinterpreted, especially by a lonely woman.

She had brought her bra in as evidence. He pulled it from the bag and dangled it in front of her.

"This looks like it has been cut with a scissors. Didn't you, in fact, remove your bra on your own so that the masseur or whatever the heck you called this guy could have better access to your skin?"

She pushed back a stray hair. "Officer, I did no such thing. I didn't get a chance to remove my clothing. He did it for me."

He slid down from the desk and stood next to her. "Your statement is filled with inconsistencies and improbabilities. Are you telling me that he gagged you, too?"

She was about to make a wisecrack when someone knocked at the door. "Sergeant, the test results came back." The young police officer handed them to the sergeant and closed the door quickly.

He snapped his pencil in two. "His DNA was not found on you in any way, shape, or form that would indicate rape. You are in major trouble here."

Then the tears came.

> That wicked bitch was ruining his life. His only defense was that this rape never happened. He

could deny it to everyone in town, but the damage was done and he was going to have to move away. He had to stay long enough to clear his name, but that could take months. How was he supposed to pay his bills in the meantime? He'd pack up most of his belongings and get out of his lease. That should be easy. They wouldn't want a rapist for a tenant, now would they? Maybe he could rent a room in Mrs. Marple's boarding house.

The phone rang. "Steven Crane?" The voice was husky and hesitant.

"Yeah. Who's this?"

"It's Officer Mangelli. The report came back and there's no evidence of your DNA on your accuser. We're sorry, but we have to follow up on all complaints. You're free to continue living your life as you were before this happened." He cleared his throat. "Shit happens, Crane. Don't let this little episode in your life define you."

Steven hung up the phone. He was seething. Define me? Is this guy crazy? He's as nuts as she is! The papers denounced me, I can't get a job in my field, and I feel like I have post-traumatic stress disorder. No, pre-traumatic, current-traumatic, and post-traumatic stress all rolled into one. He had been regarded as guilty and she had seen to ruining his life. This was a nightmare and he wasn't sure he could awaken from it. Sweat appeared on his forehead and he reached for a tissue at the same time as he grabbed for his cell. He could multitask, but not massage and rape at the same time.

He would try to reach Stuart once again.

THE BALL IS IN YOUR COURT

The weather was finally warming and Stella was so happy to take the time to enjoy a tennis game. Cassandra had come in for a long weekend because Stella was finally going to have her boutique opening this Saturday.

She could certainly take out a few hours to work off some steam. There had been endless hours at her desk planning for this day and it would go off without a hitch. Maybe even Stuart would stop by to see her crowning glory. Stella would mention it before they met Cassandra for dinner this evening. Stuart had raged when she told him she was finally opening her boutique. He had acted like a little boy and *what did you do when a little boy was having a tantrum? Walk away!* Her friend was staying at a nearby hotel, having refused an invitation to stay at their house. "I have bad habits, Stella. I'm a slob and I go to sleep very late and I'd just rather meet up with you," she said. "Listen, I hear my call waiting. Let me know when we're getting together. We will see each other before Saturday, yes?"

She unzipped the sports bag to reach for her tennis racquet while she waited for Cassandra. The sun was out and it was a perfect spring day with just a subtle breeze. She adjusted her pleated white skirt and pulled her matching white top down. She bent to tighten the laces on her sneaks and began to stretch.

Cassandra drove her car onto West Forty-Fifth Avenue toward Ninth Avenue in Manhattan. She would take the New Jersey turnpike and get to the hotel near Gladwyne in about two and a half hours. Traffic was heavy no matter what time of the day a person tried to leave Manhattan. She had learned how to zip in and out of the cars throughout the city, but it would still take time to get to her friend's house.

She loved living in Manhattan and still had some modeling jobs even though her boutique kept her very busy. The jobs were getting slimmer just like the young models. Thank goodness for her store. Cassandra had good employees and they always covered for her. Things were going well and her clientele enjoyed her upscale clothing and accessories. Her husband was very tolerant of the long hours. Thank goodness she was able to afford a nanny for the kids.

She was excited for her friend, Stella, and couldn't wait to see her new store. If she had the same luck as Cassandra, the customers would flock to her as well.

Stella's name should mean something to some of the savvy customers.

She looked forward to seeing Stella. Cassandra loved her. Not in the way of a woman romantically loving another woman, but as a true friend. A huge smile filled Cassandra's face as she thought of her friend. They had worked together in the modeling field and had been each other's support system in a business filled with beautiful people with very ugly ways about them. They had been each other's rock until Stella married Stuart and dropped out of her career to devote time to him. How backward she could be! She thought to herself how the adage about taking the girl away from the farm but not the farm away from the girl rang so true! Stella was smart, but still small-town. It had been great to see her when they had both come to Anne's funeral. It had been way too long and now she looked forward to seeing her friend again. The radio blared and Cassandra would sing all the way to Philly.

"Yesterday, yesterday seems so far away…" Her voice carried out of the window and she turned the volume up louder.

"Cassandra! Over here! I'm ready for a competition, not only at tennis, but at whose shop does the best! Only kidding!" Stella laughed out loud. "How are you?" She hugged her friend with both arms wrapped around her beautifully slim back and slid her arm through Cassandra's as she walked her onto the court. It had been a while since Stella had seen her but she hadn't forgotten how beautiful she was. Her hair was long and silky and blonde like Stella's and she had pulled it back into a ponytail for the game. Cassandra was taller than Stella, perhaps six feet tall in stocking feet and as graceful as a gazelle. They had been two peas in a pod after their first meeting at a photo shoot. It seemed so long ago.

"Where's your luggage? I hope you have changed your mind about staying here!"

Cassandra put her tennis bag on the bench. "I already checked into my hotel. Let's play ball!"

They stretched their long legs against the net. "You're doing okay for yourself, Stella. I hope you're happy. I can't wait to see the house and see Stuart tonight," she said, as she brought her racquet across her chest and swiftly swept it into the air. "It's a perfect day for a tennis game. Let's do it."

"Okay, love-love. Let me change that score right away with a brilliant serve!" Cassandra laughed.

On the other side of the net, a teary-eyed Stella burst into full-blown tears.

"Oh, dear. You can't be that upset that I'll win the game! What's going on with you, Stella?" She dropped the racquet onto the court and jogged around to the other side.

Stella went to her tennis bag and searched for a tissue. "It's just that when you said love-love, I went immediately into my crybaby state. It's really nothing, Cassandra." She plopped down on the bench and motioned for Cassandra to sit next to her.

"I'm sorry, Cassandra. You didn't drive all this way to listen to me cry. She dabbed at her eyes, blew her nose, and ditched the tissue in the trashcan by the bench. "But Stuart has just been acting like an ass lately, and with the opening of my new boutique, everything is just affecting my nerves."

"Honey, we don't have to play tennis or, for that matter, any games. We're friends. I came here from New York to support you and if it isn't all about your new shop, I'll still support you any way I can. Is your marriage in trouble?" Cassandra took another tissue and dabbed at Stella's wet cheeks.

"It's just that he's been so inattentive. And uncaring too. When I mentioned the boutique to him, he was completely disinterested. After some thought on his part, he roared like a lion. He screamed and carried on and all of a sudden he became very interested. Interested in himself. How would poor Stuart look without his wife always at his disposal? Cassandra, I gave up my career for him. He's not interested in having babies right now—those are his words—and he wants me to be available to him whenever he calls or comes home. I feel like another one of his employees. Or more like an underpaid hooker!"

The trees surrounding the tennis court began to sway in the light breeze and Cassandra patted her friend's hand. "Maybe he's just too focused on his practice. It can't be easy to be a partner wondering all the time how much money they can bring in to support the partners and their staff. C'mon, dry those big eyes of yours and let me be the one to bring you down with a wicked game of tennis!"

PASS THE SALT OR MAKE A PASS?

The three of them had dinner at a lovely little restaurant in the area of the hotel where Cassandra was staying. The old stone inn was charming. There was a fireplace and a beautifully appointed dining room, where a group of people from the Main Line were sprinkled like salt and pepper throughout the main room. She thought to herself that Stuart couldn't be as bad as Stella had said. He joined them for dinner, didn't he? Stella must have just been having a bad moment. Although Stuart was certainly a take-charge kind of guy, as he ordered the wine without asking either of them what they might like, and when the waiter appeared to take their order, he actually ordered for them!

"I'll make it easy for you, fella." Stuart looked up at the waiter and smiled. "All three of us will have the calamari to start, Caesar salad, rack of lamb medium, and instead of the mashed potatoes, put some fingerlings on the plate."

Cassandra and Stella locked eyes and both reached for the bread basket at the same time. They both bit into their steaming rolls at the same moment. If they stuffed their mouths then aggression wouldn't pour out. When they had been models together, they watched every morsel of food that passed their lips, but now they would enjoy the taste of each bite in spite of Stuart.

After the entrée was served, they ate eagerly. "Stella, remember the days when we could only take a bite of whatever was in front of us? We had to stay emaciated for the cameras and we were always starving! We would eat mints not just for our breath, but we always thought they fortified us!" They both laughed.

Stuart interjected, "It behooves you ladies to continue to stay in shape. No one wants a fat girl!" He laughed too, but he was alone in his little joke. The two friends simultaneously took a lamb chop and earnestly bit into it. Stella used her napkin and excused herself from the table to head for the ladies' room.

"She's beautiful, isn't she?" Cassandra asked Stuart.

"Not as pretty as you. You have the most beautiful hair. A guy wouldn't mind running his fingers through it," he stated smugly.

She tried to switch the conversation back to Stella. "She could still be anything she wants to be. She was blossoming as a model when she married you and she's still young enough to go back to it, but this boutique will put her on the map again, I'm sure." Cassandra turned to see if Stella was coming back.

"I'm not interested in discussing her little plan." Stuart raised his voice slightly.

Cassandra looked at him in disbelief. "Surely you are invited to the opening tomorrow! Stella mentioned that you might be coming."

He put his napkin down on the table. "I'd rather meet up with you while she's busy. What do you say?" He stretched his fingers out to reach hers.

She recoiled, repulsed by the thought. "First of all, I'm married and so are you. Secondly, she's my friend and your wife. Don't be an ass, Stuart!"

"What are you two up to?" Stella slid into her chair before Stuart could even consider standing to help. "You both look like the cat who swallowed the canary!"

Cassandra tried to make small conversation, but she was seething. She tried to hide her feelings from her friend, but her mind was racing as to how to get a moment alone with Stella in order to tell her about her obnoxious husband. What was it that someone had said to her one day? If you would find a friend's husband cheating on her, would you tell her? She had found it difficult to answer then. But right now, she was angry enough to tell Stella. Just as Stuart was trying to betray Stella, wouldn't Cassandra be betraying Stella if she held her tongue? Maybe those tears on the court were a river dammed up, just waiting to overflow. He had turned out to be such a jerk.

"Pass the salt, Stuart," she said, a little too forcefully.

FASHIONATION

"Not now, Cat-a-Comb! I have to get ready!" Stella shooed him away from her legs. She sat in front of the vanity mirror, staring at herself, and wondered if she could pull off a successful business even with such hard work to get it started. She ran the brush through her hair and held the hand mirror to the back of her head to see if it was perfect. She took her fingers and gently pulled back the corner of her eyes. She couldn't be having crow's feet at her age, could she? She pushed away the thought and went to her closet to grab for her little black dress with the satin piping. Stella slid into the perfect size two and smiled at the thought that she was still the same size as she was before she married Stuart. No pregnancies, lots of exercise, and being careful with her intake of food had allowed her to continue to keep her model's figure. She had actually put on a few pounds after she stopped modeling, but she was still able to keep fit. A little extra dab of perfume and she was ready for the world.

There was to be a ribbon-cutting ceremony directly in front of the store, where buyers lined up like good soldiers against the right side of the second floor of the mall and its famous anchor store, Neiman Marcus. It was a great location and although the last shop located there had failed, Stella knew she would not allow that to happen. She was fully prepared and had extra funds to infuse into the business should they be needed. Stuart had finally succumbed and cosigned the lease. He was available for extra money needed to infuse into the business. Between the bank loan and her own funds to back her up, she was ready. Asking Stuart for money for the store would be her last choice. But it was far better to have both names on everything. Wasn't it?

Cassandra was advertised as the celebrity attending the opening and, bless her, she showed up right on time. She was dressed to the hilt and wore glamour like she had the copyright on it. She kept objecting to being the celebrity, constantly affirming that the real celebrity was the owner herself.

Customers were browsing and running their hands all over the merchandise like a bunch of caterpillars, creeping over the cashmere and cotton. It had taken Stella and her assistant hours of preparation, folding and hanging the clothes, dressing the window mannequins, and advertising the opening. She had announced a door prize and for anyone who spent five hundred dollars that day, there was an added perk thrown in. The crowd went on with their search, acting like detectives looking for clues. They fingered the buttons on the cardigans and swept their hands down the draped and pleated dresses and skirts. Cassandra mingled, encouraging as many women as she could to buy. Couldn't they consider their purchases an investment? Badgley Mishka, Diane Von Furstenberg, Missoni, Ralph Lauren—who wouldn't want to own something from these brilliant designers? Stella's few years in the modeling business gave her the clout to connect with these major fashion designers.

Manola Blahnik shoes sat waiting patiently in the dressing room so that the customer could see what her outfit would look like put together. Six-inch heels pointed to each woman as she entered her private dressing room.

After hours of people strolling in and out, it was time to have the drawing and give away the designer watch for some lucky shopper.

Number 43. The shriek could be heard down the mall! A young woman of no more than eighteen had won! "Do you have your receipt? I'd like to see if you spent at least five hundred dollars so you can win the extra gift," Stella said with excitement in her voice. This young girl had spent a thousand and Stella wasn't about to lecture her on the perils of too much spending. She was so thrilled to win both prizes (the other being a bag of makeup goodies) and Stella was hopeful she would tell all of her friends and the mothers of her friends. This could be an inexpensive way to advertise very expensive attire.

Even her next-door neighbor had come to her opening and the day had been a huge success. Stella sat on the stool at the cash register and counted the cash and receipts. This was exceptional. If it could continue like this, she jokingly thought to herself, Stuart could retire!

"Stella, I need a few minutes of your time. I know you are exhausted, but I'm driving home in the morning and I want to discuss something with you," Cassandra held Stella's chin in order to keep her focused.

"You were an angel to do this, Cassandra. Everyone who walked in here was drooling over your beauty. You helped make the opening a huge success and I can't thank you enough for coming to Philly when you have so much of your own stuff to do in New York." She fondly touched her friend's hands and dragged a bridge chair over to the counter so she could sit next to her.

"This isn't private enough. Can we go back to your office for a minute before I leave?"

"Stella! Everything here was perfect. I loved the weekend and thank you so much for hosting me. Great tennis, great dinner, great boutique. But not so great a husband." She turned her head away so she couldn't look her in the eyes.

"Oh, Cassandra. He couldn't be here. He tried. Stuart's always so busy. Don't worry too much about it," she gripped the receipts in her hand.

"I'm not talking about that." Cassandra paused. *Although he could have been here for you, Stella.* "I'm referring to dinner last night. When you went to the ladies' room, he flirted with me. I hesitated to tell you, but I think you should know such a thing. He's a bit of a cad and you should watch for the first hint of trouble. I'm sorry to spoil your wonderful day." An awkward silence fell between them until Stella's assistant came into the back office. "Excuse me. We're getting ready to close for the day and another customer just walked in!"

JUST SAY GOOD KNIGHT

Clive's getting a little sloppy lately, Stuart thought. He wasn't the slightest bit apprehensive about handing over the financial controls to him and hadn't asked one question. *Thank goodness he trusts me.*

He was so happy that he was a whiz at the computer. He didn't have to rely on Cotton and worry about her nose being in his business. She was good for the business of sex and he had made sure she was available to him whenever he wanted and needed her. But on the subject of the law firm, she could stay completely out of the loop unless he absolutely needed her help. He would create a file for a fictitious employee and pay her a salary that he could easily pocket. Why, he'd even create a fake social security number for her. No one would refer to it. At the end of the year, payroll would issue tax forms to a fake PO address for a fake employee. Who would question his authority? Payroll would release a check without question. There were so many employees now that they couldn't possibly know everyone. He would set up a direct deposit account in her name. He typed a name at the top of the page: Donna Quick. He laughed to himself. *She'll be a great asset to the firm!*

He put his feet up on his desk causing the different papers to slide like they were on thin ice. His mind wandered to Stelli. He only had a brief moment with Cassandra to try to seduce her. Damn Stelli for coming back from the bathroom so fast! As much as he loved women, he sure didn't want to be in a crowded boutique with them. She'd just have to get over the fact that he didn't come to her opening. It would probably fail anyway. What did she know about business? She hadn't worked for several years and even then, everything had been taken care of for her. Models were princesses and always treated royally. She had never quite made it to the top of her profession, but that didn't stop her small entourage from doting on her. True, a few top designers knew her name and she was probably on the brink of model stardom when he met her. Their relationship developed very quickly and he was able to take over as her lawyer and guide her as he wanted things to happen. He negotiated her contracts and handled the paper trail in the direction of her fame, mostly in pretense. He didn't actually want her to succeed. Stuart pivoted his chair and stared out the window at the world moving below.

When he came along, he became her prince in shining armor, and played the game of encouraging her, all the while whisking her away from the limelight. He should have been the center of her universe. She had promised! How dare she stray from that responsibility! He was sick of her behavior. It had been a poor choice to marry such an annoying girl. He snapped the chair back like it was a stick of bubble gum, his thoughts blowing hot air. He would continue to build an untroubled relationship with Cotton, who would be easier to manipulate. She adored him and would do exactly as he said.

THE SECRET KEEPER

Steven hadn't been able to reach his brother. Stuart either told him he was too busy to talk or he was unreachable. The room was dark and he lay there in bed with a bad headache. Every time he called Stuart and didn't get anywhere with him, he would think back to their childhood.

Thank goodness their mom had finally purchased bunk beds for the twins. He would hear Stuart talking in his sleep and if he had been right beside him, it would have kept him up all night. Stuart, naturally, took the top bunk. It was more fun to climb the ladder and fantasize that he was a pirate ascending his ship than it was to lie on the bottom bunk. But Steven would escape the room faster when the talking in his brother's sleep got too annoying. He would walk down to the living room, making certain he didn't squeak on the stairs and wake up his mother. Lucky for him, he didn't have any more siblings to contend with.

Most times it took a lot more than sleep talking to bother Steven. He had the misfortune of trying to share secrets with his twin and often they backfired on him. One time he had been so angry with Stuart. They had been walking to school and he confessed that he had a crush on this girl in their class. He swore his brother to secrecy.

"Don't say a word about it, Stuart." He winked. "Let's do the secret handshake on it." He had reached out and curled his hand in a fist, and Stuart had met his fist with a meaningful and trusting bump.

The next day Steven walked the tree-lined path to the front of the school. Stuart had faked a stomachache so that he could get out of a math test. There was no way Steven would miss an exam. He always had to work harder than his brother to make the grades. He didn't want to be set back and have to worry about rescheduling or even being given a failing mark. He smoothed his T-shirt as he climbed the steps to the gaping door, a big mouth swallowing up the kids. Excited about seeing his crush in the hallway going to and from classes, he rushed to homeroom.

He slid into the hard chair before he felt the tap on his shoulder. When he turned around, there she was. She wasn't in their homeroom. Why was she here today?

Her red hair flamed around her freckled face and he thought he would melt from her fire.

"Steven? That is your name, isn't it? You're the twin that your brother told me about." She stood there above him and he couldn't get up. He felt frozen to his wooden seat. "I'm going to the prom with your brother and I just wanted to say don't play any pranks on me that night and try to switch: I kinda like your brother.

Sssshhh." She put her finger to her rosy lips. Another secret? That louse had listened to him talk about his crush on her and went to the school yesterday and asked her to the prom.

"Yeah, sure. Don't worry. I wouldn't want to imitate my brother." He shoved his pencil behind his ear.

He scratched his head as if he were trying to pull the thoughts out of his brain. He had been so angry with Stuart and that day he had vowed that that would be the last school they attended together. Maybe his mother would listen to reason. He would plead with her to go to a different school. He would apply to as many colleges as possible until he found one his brother didn't want to go to. Would his mom even allow it? She was always so intent on them being together. Could he break away from being tied to Stuart?

The mountain of catalogues from the different colleges suddenly became insurmountable. His mother had insisted that they go to the same college; they would take care of each other. In a fit of disgust, he dumped in the trash all the information he had collected from the universities and surrendered to his mother's wishes.

He studied physical therapy and Stuart took classes for prelaw. At Thanksgiving each year, Steven had brought home a different girl from school, making sure he always befriended the loneliest of his female classmates. He would dangle them in front of Stuart, proving that he could get any girl he wanted.

During their junior year, Steven had brought home a beautiful sophomore, whose family was living in England at the time. She was alone and lonely and he had met her at the activities center on campus and dated her a couple of times. He would ask her to come to his home for the holiday. Even though the holidays at his house were kept very simple because there was always a shortage of money, his mom made sure to create the best possible experience. There might be a new stepfather at the holiday table, but she would put up the pretenses, along with the turkey. The only oddity was the empty chair always placed at the table when they celebrated. Was it for his absent father? The twins always thought it was strange, but neither felt comfortable asking about it.

"She's a beauty, Steven. Where'd you get her from?" Stuart shoved his twin playfully.

"You better lay off, Stuart. I'm dating her and let's not have a misunderstanding. Keep your hands off!" He not-so-playfully shoved him back.

Martie had slept on the old sofa that night and Steven and Stuart had gone to their childhood bunk beds. In the middle of the night, Steven felt the rattle of the ladder as Stuart climbed down from his perch. "Probably thirsty," he had muttered to himself.

It didn't take long in the morning for him to hear from his twin that they had done the nasty right on their mom's couch in the middle of the night.

Steven was the stronger of the two, but gentle in so many other ways. But he was not going to let his brother taunt him. Stuart had a radically inverted morality, never caring what the consequences of his actions would be. How dare he steal Martie from right under his nose?

The three of them were sitting around the kitchen table just taking in the smell of the bacon their mom was frying up in the pan. Stuart kept sneering at Steven and Martie kept twirling her hair around in her fingers. It was the color of the fire under the frying pan. Steven was entranced. *He loved redheads*. He smirked and thought to himself, *I definitely have a thing for redheads!* All of a sudden, he snapped out of his reverie and remembered how Stuart had moved in on his girl.

Steven skid the kitchen chair out from under the table and got up and slugged Stuart.

Mom turned. "What is going on? I've only got the two of you now. Please try to be nice to each other!"

The image was clear to Steven as he thought back to that time. "What did she mean about *only* having the two of them *now*? Had she been stifling her thoughts about their father and were they finally seeping out of her?

He pushed himself up on his elbows. Anytime he had been in a fight to defend himself, if Stuart had been present, he always stood by laughing. He never came to his assistance.

I'LL TAKE MINE
WITH A LUMP OF SUGAR

She had felt the lump when showering. That was what she told the doctor. How could this be happening to someone so young? This was not a good time, but then when was a good time? The freaking out, the mammogram, the biopsy, the waiting for results—it was all too much. She was still wrapped in her bath towel when she called the doctor. He was a thorough man, up-to-date on all the standards of care and knew all the algorithms. He would take care of her.

He had sent her for a biopsy and she entered the women's center nervously, with her thoughts racing. Two Lorazepams had just about taken the edge off of her jumpiness and she felt like she just wanted to put her head down and pull the covers up. No lump, no business worries, no nagging concerns about Stuart—just a peaceful sleep.

Stella had been taken back to one of the operating rooms and the nurse had asked her to lay face down on the table with her arms at her sides. One breast was pulled to one side, while the other was swallowed up by a hole in the table. The machine clamped the sides of her breast together, ready to make mashed potatoes out of her body. The doctor inserted the needle to numb her and at that point she didn't care what was done to her.

"Hang in there, Stella. Almost done." The doctor patted her gently on the shoulder.

Stella felt some suction in and out of her breast, like the arms of a vending machine dropping a product down and pulling back to its resting place. Up and down, in and out, in and out, and then it was over.

She went back to work the next day and tried to keep busy, but her mind drifted to the biopsy results and the what-ifs. She put a smile on her face for the customers, almost looking like an artist who had painted a slice of red, happy lips on her face.

When the phone rang two days later, Stella could hardly breathe. It could have been anyone calling, but the doctor had said results would be in two days from the biopsy and the song that played when her cell rang jangled her nerves with each note. Happy music. Would the outcome of this call be happy?

"Hi, this is Stella," she spoke with hesitance.

"This is Dr. Matthews, Stella. I don't have the best of news for you, unfortunately, but I think we're going to have to do a lumpectomy and let's arrange that as quickly as possible." The doctor spoke quickly with shots of words coming out of his mouth like a stun gun. *Oh, yes,* Stella thought, *it is stunning me and dropping me to my knees.*

"Doctor, I'm so young. This is not fair." She could hear the whiny sound of her voice.

The pause on the phone was deafening until the doctor finally spoke. "Honey, nothing is fair about this, but I feel sure we will get it all. Let's just get it over with. I'll put my assistant on so we can schedule you."

THE AUDIT

He was sweating. He reached for the handkerchief he kept in his pocket and wiped away the beads that formed a parade on his forehead. He would never use the pocket square that was perfectly arranged in his suit jacket. He had an image to portray and he would do so elegantly. Stuart needed a break. The work was starting to get to him and the coke he had begun to snort was costing him a fortune, but not as much as the bad run he was having with gambling. Stelli was piling up bills too. "Damn it!" He slammed his fist down on the desk and rubbed away the soreness with his other hand. Cotton had gone on vacation and he was annoyed that she wasn't around to ease his pain and stress. She hadn't been that easy to control, after all. Stuart had begged her to wait until he was free to go on a vacation together, but she was smarter than he thought. She had said, "Stuart, that could be never, unless you divorce your wife." He wanted to take in her smell and breathe in a heavenly aroma unlike the coke he normally inhaled. She had told him the name of her perfume was Man Killer and it sure slew him! He needed another hit, but he had to concentrate on the paperwork. If he made one mistake, that would be the end of him.

Clive called him in to his private office for a short meeting. Stuart was not having a good day and this was a bad time to interrupt him for who knows what trivial matter he wanted to discuss. Sometimes Clive could be so anal and he would worry about every single detail. *Well, he had certainly missed Stuart's little escapades! He had two partners. Couldn't he bother Joe Yelds? What was Clive so worried about?*

"Please sit down, Stuart, and thanks for popping in." Clive stood to shake his hand as though he hadn't seen him in weeks.

"Clive, what's up?" Stuart draped himself on the black leather sofa instead of sitting formally on one of the chairs opposite Clive's desk.

"Let's get our ducks in order, Stuart." He began to subconsciously line up his pens and pencils, putting them into position as if they were toy soldiers. "We are going to be audited. It could take weeks, but they'll be here every day. Glad I could depend on you to handle the finances. Not a thing to worry about!" The sun was dropping in like an unwanted visitor and Clive got up and drew the blinds closed.

Supply and demand. Supply and demand. This was the economy they were dealing with. The legal market was inundated with lawyers who saw how much an attorney could make and they wanted in. Then, all of a sudden, there are too many and the pay had to come down. They had hired young attorneys right out of law school. Did they think they were going to make the same kind of money as the partners?

Well, they could audit their little hearts out. Stuart's pay wasn't going to budge. He deserved all of this, didn't he? He should have a bonus for all the hard work he was doing. He shouldn't have to put up with this crap just because he was the junior partner.

He went back to his own office and slammed the door behind him. Audit? *Holy shit!* His mind raced. He paced. The stupid drugs were impeding his thinking. He shouldn't worry, should he? This was routine and he had covered his tracks. No small-minded accountant could trace any wrongdoing. Stuart needed a trace of coke to get through today.

The handkerchief was swiftly yanked out of his pocket as if he were trying to do a magic trick. It fluttered in the air from the lined pocket to his lined face.

It was a government audit. What the hell? What were they up to? When Clive had called Stuart into his office (*and, by the way, where was the other partner?*) he hadn't alluded to any trouble. A simple audit. This was more than Stuart bargained for. Nothing was simple about an audit. They were questioning $446,000 in billings, a hefty portion of the firm's expenses. It was a good thing Stuart had barely scratched the surface of his ideas for embezzling. That number would have grown.

Mail fraud? Tax evasion? It wasn't unusual for law firms to have their costs questioned or disallowed by government auditors, often for accounting matters like allocation of photocopying expenses and billing documentation. The audit of their law firm would certainly include some of those kinds of questions. But they were breathing down their necks now and the IRS would surely say that some of the charges in question were unusual. The room began to spin as his mind began to race.

Stuart had submitted bills for participating in depositions when he never attended any sessions. *That was common practice, wasn't it?* Stuart thought. *Would they pick up on the other ways he was milking the firm?* He felt like he was going to throw up. He needed a hit badly. He patted his pocket hoping he still had some coke left and came up empty. He unlocked his personal drawer and moved his Blackberry, looking under it. He shoved aside some photos taken of him and Stelli on their honeymoon. The pictures had been put in there so that Cotton wouldn't have Stelli staring at her when they were all over each other. No coke. Damn.

He had to focus on the audit. He snapped his fingers in front of his face as if to check and see if he was still awake.

The fake invoices? The fake employees supposedly hired by him? He had prided himself on his ability to hire companies to do certain work for the law firm. It had been so easy. Everyone was on the take. They were perfectly willing to give him a kickback for the job he hired them for. They did the job. Oh, yes. He smirked to himself. But they didn't put any effort in to it. He had hired a cleaning service to come in after hours and clean the offices. The head honcho gave Stuart a nice amount of money as his way of saying thanks for giving us the job over the other bids. Every morning when he entered through the company's front door, he could easily spot the work that hadn't been done. No one had said a word. The attorneys were doing their dirty work every day and weren't interested in how dirty their offices might be. Now the accountants were going to look at all the dust bunnies that had collected because of him. He had personally dirtied everything and they were about to sweep him onto the sidewalk and maybe even into a jail cell. His stomach turned. He pulled the trash basket closer.

THE CLEANUP

The hurricane struck with such force. It was so unusual for the Eastern Seaboard to get hit like that. It had been two decades since such high winds and heavy rains came to the area. The shore had been evacuated, but Stella had no time to plan a ride to the house to see about any damages. Anyway, they wouldn't even let her onto the road leading into Ventnor.

On the Main Line, she was plunged into darkness just like most of the homes in her area. Trees had turned into projectiles and had caused several deaths. A relentless march to the region had begun and would not end for several hours. Airlines had canceled flights along the East Coast. Trains and buses suspended service. The hurricane caused historic flooding. A picture-perfect leafy suburb was now dotted with generators giving off the pungent odor of gasoline on every street. The neighbors would lose their frozen foods and flooded basements would abound.

Stella did not know what to do with herself. The mall was closed and, of course, her boutique was as well.

She had spoken to her employees and they had agreed to cover for her while she would be in the hospital and comforted her by promising to take care of everything. She had received a call from the hospital rescheduling her lumpectomy for the following week after the cleanup from the storm. The wait would be hell.

She had placed her household tools in a basket and went around the big house with a duster, window cleaner, and furniture spray and had cleaned every speck of dust. Stella pulled back the curtains to let enough light in so she could move about the house freely. The housekeeper would not be able to get there for a few weeks. The cleaning would be a temporarily therapeutic distraction from what was facing her.

Stella sang at the top of her lungs as she shifted from one room to the other, trying to keep her mind from racing to the possibilities that faced her. Her own noise and the whistling winds temporarily blocked out the horrible thoughts that kept creeping into her mind.

When she finally sat down exhausted from her chores, Cat-a-comb, who hid under the sofa while she sang at a high pitch, magically appeared and jumped into her lap and, like a newborn baby, sniffed at her breast. She remembered that he had done this several times before her diagnosis and it had never dawned on her that it meant anything. He loved to wrap himself around Stella when she slept and animals sniffed all the time, didn't they?

Could animals sense cancer? Why hadn't this been a sign for her to go to the doctor sooner? One night Cat-a-comb had climbed into their bed and took his paw and dragged it down her breast. He had sniffed at her and meowed as if to tell her something. Was he feeling sorry for her because she hadn't had sex in so long? The cat kept at it and had seemed adamant that something was there. Now, in retrospect, she visualized him with a stethoscope around his neck. Stella had read that cats could sense the disease. In recent months, she had read an article in the paper about a cat who lived in a nursing home and he would survey his kingdom with a sharp eye, cuddling up to patients moments before they met their Maker. Was there credibility to the theory that he sensed their imminent demise? There could be a noxious or sweet odor triggering their investigation of the patients. Stella had a diagnostic aid living right under her roof and she had paid absolutely no attention to him other than to give his warm fur a quick pat before turning over to go to sleep. Stuart was often out like a light long before the light was off. He couldn't have discovered the lump, could he? He was far too disinterested in sex these days.

The warm afghan wrapped around her body like a snake and the cat snuggled cozily. Was she losing Stuart? She was still young and beautiful. Her body weight hadn't changed since they married. In the beginning of her career, she had vigorously exercised, but she had given that boring activity up very quickly. Most of the models starved themselves, but she grew up on a farm with her mom's home cooking. How could she give up all those delicious comfort foods in order to be skinny? Stella thought, *How lucky I am to be naturally thin!*

Now, would losing her breast reduce her even further?

The winds raged outside and the storm continued within her.

CHEMICAL WARFARE

He had to go gamble. He would tell Stelli that he would take the drive to the shore to check on the house now that the storm had abated. The crazy weather had held him back from going to the casino. He was getting low on drugs and had tried to call his dealer only to find out that the phone service had been cut. A dealer could easily be found in Atlantic City. He stood up from his den chair and began to take measured steps from one side of the room to the other, one deliberate advance at a time. Perspiration formed on his brow. His toe caught the end of the sofa and he yelped. Stuart had to get out of there. Stella was cleaning the house and they both were going nuts locked in a prison of selfish concern for themselves.

She had interrupted his train of thought the other night when she spat out the words about needing surgery on her breast. That was one more thing he had to deal with. She would be imperfect after the surgery and it would be more reason for him to turn to Cotton and any other cutie that crossed his path. His wife wasn't that interesting anyway. She had gone against him when she opened the boutique and there had been a few times when he needed to prance her around his firm's social circle and his clients' parties. He was mixing with some very rich people and he had married Stella to show her off. She would surely impress them all with her beauty. But no, she was not interested in circulating with people she hardly knew. She was becoming of little use to Stuart and it was embarrassing to have to explain what she did for a living now. He had cosigned with her on her little venture in a moment of weakness. He had done too much coke that day and wasn't operating on all cylinders.

Couldn't he just financially support her? Why did she have to work? She had saved some money from her modeling days and wasn't that enough to satisfy her? That was part of their deal, wasn't it? Stay home and be ready for your husband at all times. She just couldn't get it right. And now, she expected him to be at her beck and call with surgery when he had to be at work. They'd be offering her chemicals of a different kind. He was putting things into his body that made him very happy. They'd be taking things out of her body. The thought reviled him.

He was trying to cover his ass with the problems the auditors were creating for him and he didn't have time to worry about another part of the body, especially hers. She could get a friend to drive her to the hospital.

Maybe this time he would call his brother and let him know how sad he was feeling about Stella. Stuart could set the stage so that Steven thought he was needed by his twin brother.

Steven had not attended their wedding. The day that Stella and Stuart were to get married, he had called and congratulated them. Stella had told him they were getting married and he felt it was the proper thing to at least call.

Stuart was not interested in his brother being there or their mom attending, for that matter. And their father was nowhere to be found anyway. How many stepfathers had there been? No, he wasn't interested in including a person who was almost a stranger to him. They were unsophisticated people and would only embarrass him. He would surround himself with friends of his own choosing and it would be a perfect day.

If Stella hadn't mentioned the wedding to Stuart's brother, he wouldn't have balked for the longest time as to why he hadn't been invited. Stuart hadn't needed him to mess up anything with his stupid comments and he had placated him by saying it would just be a small wedding—no family, no friends. He had bought that story and wished them well and any time Stuart spoke to him after the marriage, which wasn't often, he danced around any specifics. There might be a time in the future that Steven would come in handy, but that hadn't been one of them. Steven had always wanted what his twin had: success, a beautiful wife, his brother's life. They had always been separate since the day they popped out of their mother's womb. They were never a unit even though everyone referred to them as *the twins*. Their minds were different; their bodies were different. Stuart smirked at the thought. His brother had always felt as though Stuart had ripped them apart from one another as if Steven had been a delicate fabric to cut away and discard, strips of DNA thrown in the trash. Well, he had been right. He shrugged his shoulders as if someone were in the room with him. *What the hell do I care about that imbecile?*

PLAN B

Steven would set up shop on his own in a new town. He would get away, as far away as possible, from the ugly events that had surrounded him and the name he had built for himself as a masseur, only for it to be destroyed as if he were an old building being detonated. He would have to rebuild his name as if it were a new house, brick by brick, one performance at a time, with customer satisfaction his goal. He couldn't wait to get back in the game.

This time would be different. He would not answer to a boss; he would *be* the boss. He would pay rent in a storefront operation that invited clients to come through the door and pay for his services. He would even hire employees and set up several private rooms and create a spa-like environment for men and women. For the first time in weeks, he felt excited about the future. He had a vision. It would take money, but he would persist until his brother would be interested in making an investment. The bank would give him a loan. There had to be an angle. He would make it happen.

Or maybe, just maybe, he would hang out a shingle as a chiropractor. Who would be the wiser? Who would check his credentials? His hand went to his mouth as if to stifle a laugh. He could purchase a shingle on the Internet so easily.

He would get hold of his brother and tell him of his plans. Now if he could only reach him.

THE WORST YEAR OF HER LIFE AND THE BREAST

Cassandra came to give Stella support. She couldn't understand why that bastard husband of hers wouldn't be her champion at a time like this. He was so self-centered and egotistical, not to mention he was a lousy husband. Stella had gotten in over her head when she married him and Cassandra was going to be her support system no matter what it took. No one should have to suffer alone. She squeezed Stella's hand.

Stella's surgeon drew markings on her breast to show where the incision would be made. She watched as the felt-tip marker came down on her flesh. Maybe he would draw a clown face. Wasn't she in a three-ring circus with all the medical staff prancing around her? Wasn't she on a carnival ride going up and down like her life had been? An orderly pushed her stretcher into another area where the anesthesia room was located. Cassandra waved. "I'll be right here when you return."

The nurse inserted an intravenous infusion line into her arm. A medication to relax her dripped into her veins. Stella tried to think good thoughts and shook Stuart from her mind. She drifted to a place where fog had set in.

The lumpectomy surgery took less than forty minutes. A rubber tube called a drain was surgically inserted into Stella's breast area to collect excess fluid that might accumulate in the space where the tumor was. The surgeon finally stitched the incision closed and dressed the wound.

Cassandra paced in the waiting room until the doctor came out. He asked Cassandra where Stella's husband was and she had to offer up a big excuse.

"He's traveling for business, unfortunately. I'm sure he wanted to be here with her. I'm the closest person to her who could be with her today. What's the diagnosis, doctor?" she nervously questioned him.

The doctor patted her hand. "She came through the surgery with flying colors." He smiled briefly. "She won't have to deal with chemo and radiation, because the cancer didn't spread. It looks like it was contained within the lump and didn't make it to her lymph nodes. The test results will come back from the lab soon and we'll know for sure. In a lot of cases, there is a precautionary protocol and treatments are put in place, but she is a very lucky young lady!" He yanked at his tie nervously. Giving even good news seemed to unsettle him even though Cassandra understood from Stella that he had done hundreds of these surgeries before he had performed her operation. She indeed was very lucky. If she had to have cancer, she was blessed that it hadn't spread.

Cassandra drew in a deep breath and responded. "She'll be happy to hear that the cancer was taken out and I'm sure she'll do whatever it takes to make sure it never comes back again. Can I see her?" Her hand unintentionally went to the doctor's arm.

The doctor patted Cassandra's hand and said, "She's been transferred to the recovery room so they can monitor her heart rate, body temperature, and blood pressure. Give them an hour and I'll have the nurse come and get you. She'll be able to continue a path of recovery at home," he said encouragingly.

When she woke, Stella opened her eyes to her beautiful friend, sitting on the chair next to her bed in the recovery room. The doctor stopped in to check on her and to sign the discharge papers and give her instructions on how to care for her incision and a list of what to do. She scanned the directions: *1. Wash the wound gently with soap and water. 2. Don't drive for at least 24 hours after surgery. 3. No heavy lifting until incision heals.* And so on and so forth. She tried to wiggle herself into an upright position.

Cassandra plumped her pillow. "I'm going to be with you every step of the way. You are only a couple of hours away from me and I want to make sure you are okay." She grasped Stella's hand.

"Cassandra! You can't give up your life and your precious time! I'm fine. The report is excellent." She tried to sound relaxed.

"I'll come visit you. I can easily come in on the days you need someone with you." She pulled Stella's sheet up and gently smoothed it. "You might even be able to visit me in New York." She really wasn't sure how she could juggle all of these balls and keep her husband happy and the kids settled and her boutique running like a fine-tuned machine. But, for her friend, she was willing to try.

Stella was adamant. "Absolutely not, Cassandra! I can't let this interfere with your life. I will be able to manage. If I need anything, my employees will help me out and Stuart will be there for me when he can."

"Oh, Stella. Your knight in shining armor is riding away on his stallion," she tried to make it a joke. Cassandra opened her palm to offer her pain medication. The nurse had slipped it to her while Stella had slept off the anesthesia making her practically sign an affidavit swearing she wouldn't forget to give it to her.

"Help me get dressed. That will be the biggest help right now." She sat up again, unwilling to stay one more minute in that hospital bed, and dangled her legs on the side of the bed, ready to bolt.

After Cassandra left, Stella managed on her own. She had scheduled a follow-up appointment and they would remove her bandage then. The stitches would dissolve on their own. She stretched her arm up in the air and reminded herself to continue this exercise to prevent shoulder stiffness.

WHAT A DOPAMINE!

He slid back the metal lid to get his stash out and pushed the coke together to form a line. Stuart snorted the cocaine. He couldn't take a chance to heat the crack. It would produce vapors, and someone would smell it. No, he would rather inhale the cocaine powder through his nose and absorb it into his bloodstream through his nasal tissues. That would be fast enough. It was as rapid as it would be if he took it by injection. Soon it would deliver its magic to his brain and he would get intensely high. It would give him deep pleasure and his body would move a lot better with the drug's help. The excess of dopamine was responsible for the cocaine's euphoric effects. He would go and have a grand old time gambling. It was getting harder to pay for his habit, but as an abuser, he felt the need to administer the drug again and again and again. He would dig around for more money. *God, I need more and more money…*

Stuart had set up that offshore account so he'd have a cushion of money if he ever got caught, but it was getting more and more difficult to pay for his gambling, keep up the account, and maintain his lifestyle. It was exhausting. Maybe he would win at the tables. *Yes, I would win. I have to win. The auditors are idiots and they'll never discover my discrepancies.* He brushed at his gray suit to get off the excess powder. His blue-and-white striped tie had a drop too. *Damn. That would have been better up my nose than on my clothes! Hah!*

Stuart had sold his sperm and his blood in college, until one day he was tested for drugs and alcohol after he had been drinking all night with his buddies. That had been the end of that. He lifted his tie and scraped at the white spot. He couldn't sell any part of himself now. He was like a vessel filled with narcotics, ready to shipwreck at any moment. He would try other venues to make money wherever he could to keep his gambling, womanizing, and drug habit going. *Maybe I can even become a drug dealer. There's plenty of money to be made in that field!* The air traveled noisily through his nostrils as he sniffled, creating the sound of a desperate man.

He ran his fingers through his hair. Why should he care about drugs raging through his system? He sure wasn't going to make babies with Stelli right now. She had a career and cancer. That interfered with any daddy plan he might have entertained. And, God forbid, if Cotton got pregnant, well...

LIKE BROTHER, LIKE BROTHER

Chiropractic services and massage therapy services were becoming increasingly popular as an integrative health care option. Since Steven was already a licensed massage therapist, why couldn't he hang a shingle on his door telling the world he was a chiropractor? He could fake it. He didn't have time to go to school for several years and be more in debt than he already was. He'd create a certificate on the computer and design a chiropractic degree that he would frame for his future patients who would be looking for the symbol on the wall to prove his achievement. It wouldn't matter to most people as long as they saw that degree on the wall. They wouldn't even question whether the doctor had finished first or last in his class. He had a degree, didn't he? That was good enough. And all they would care about is if he could fix their chronic back pain, lower muscle pain, and any other discomfort issues associated with the spinal area. He could do those adjustments.

It didn't take that much education to figure out how to make his patients feel better. A deep tissue massage could feel just like an adjustment. Put the patient in la-la land and they wouldn't be the wiser. He'd be providing a valuable service. He'd even throw in some talks about nutrition. He'd manipulate his patients in more than one way.

He would be whatever they wanted him to be. The buttons of his baby blue shirt were unbuttoned practically to his navel and his hairy chest stood exposed. The women would fall at his feet. The role he would play would be whichever brought in the most money. Small-town, unsophisticated folk could easily be conned, couldn't they?

He could use a little coke to keep his energy level up. He had done some in college and his brother had once told him it could be very helpful to take the drug in order to juggle all the things they had to do in life. It would increase his energy, reduce his fatigue, and keep him mentally alert. Snort, snort and conquer the world. His mind drifted back to the time that his brother had been caught doing drugs. That wasn't likely to happen to him, was it? He was always more careful than Stuart.

Now, where could he get some?

HARRY HOUDINI

Harry Langhorne was a plain man. He sat at a desk all his working life and examined numbers on sheets of paper. He was balding and what little hair was left was turning prematurely white. He could use some of the color that rounded out his cheeks to tinge a coppery shade to the strands of hair that remained on his head. Big red circles made his cheeks look like the devil lived inside his mouth. At forty-six, Harry was unmarried, alone, and his numbers were his friends. He could do an audit with the precision of a doctor performing surgery. He could find the cancer in a company and shine with his bosses. That made his life bearable. His last assignment had been to review a large condo's financials and he had brought down the management with his swift talent of scrutiny. He felt like the king of auditors and as he sat at this small desk provided by the law firm of Crane, Borders, and Yelds, he rubbed his pencil up and down as if it were a phallic symbol.

The room was claustrophobic, but Harry had his attention on the numbers. When he first entered the tiny room, he thought the staff member had shown him into the broom closet. But there was a small desk with a computer, an uncomfortable swivel chair that squeaked with every movement, and a narrow table along the wall opposite the door. Four items. There wasn't a picture on the walls, which were painted a grim gray-white. But he didn't need much to bring them down. Harry straightened his polka-dotted bow tie and smiled to himself.

He would review vendor disbursement reports and begin there. Usually, if fraud had been committed, it was fairly likely that imaginary vendors would be invented and there would be fake bills representing them. Harry could sniff those out as if those documents were the finest perfumes in the land. It was fun doing a little detective work and asking questions of the staff. It made him feel important and he could get answers quickly.

The employees were like little children, unable to tell any falsehoods. If they saw something out of the ordinary they would nervously come to Poppa with the information.

There was no window in the room and Harry slid his jacket off. He didn't like being casual, but this workspace was not conducive to his business attire. He flicked a piece of dust off of the desk and continued his hunt.

Harry inspected the payroll reports and reviewed the personnel files. He targeted payroll records and expense reimbursements. He was not just a cruncher of numbers, but captain of the domain he was sent to protect. Were corporate credit cards used for personal use without authorization or repayment?

A large grin crossed Harry's face. Would he be the power that recommended termination of employment of a dishonest employee? There would be many oversights; there always were. He would catch the perpetrator or were there several guilty parties?

He took a sip of the coffee he had purchased from the vending machine. The coffee was bitter, but it would keep him awake. He hit the page down key to move on.

ANOTHER NASTY DIAGNOSIS

"What do you mean, Momma?" Stella practically yelled into the phone. "Can't take another thing on my plate." She absentmindedly twisted her hair around her finger and let it go to bounce back against her head. *Thank goodness, she did not have to lose her beautiful tresses.*

"What do *you* mean, Stella?"

She let the silence be her response for a moment until she could collect her thoughts. She opened the dishwasher and tucked the phone between her ear and shoulder so she could have her hands free. "I'm fine, Momma. What's going on with Poppa?" She slid a breakfast plate into the dishwasher and threw a fork and knife into the silverware holder.

"Honey, he's been acting strange for a long time. I took him to the doctor and he was diagnosed with Alzheimer's. Sometimes it goes unrecognized or undiagnosed in the early stages because they kept saying Daddy was just aging. But I insisted on testing, Stella, and that's what they told me. They did a series of tests on him and used different tools to evaluate his thinking, behavior, and physical function."

Stella sat on the kitchen stool and tried to stay calm. "What kind of tests?"

"I don't know them all, honey, but they called one a 'clock drawing test' and they conducted a health history and physical exam. Your Poppa carried on through the whole evaluation. They claim there are two types of treatments to manage it; one is using some kind of inhibitor and the other is using another chemical that helps learning and memory. He's already started on it; I think it's called Aricept, and he seems a little less confused. But Stella, running the farm is going to be a struggle. I'm not sure what we'll do." Her mom coughed, like she was trying to force the words from her lips.

Stella slid off the stool and wiped the counter, busying herself with mundane tasks while having this conversation with her mother. She had to find a way to tell her about her own medical news. Her neck began to hurt from balancing the phone between her ear and shoulder.

She brushed a crumb from the blueberry muffin she had eaten for breakfast and flicked it into the sink. "What are some of Poppa's symptoms?"

She heard her mother take a deep breath. "He's become more argumentative than ever. He's even started wandering around the house at night and won't remember any of it afterwards. And, he wandered over there, you know, by the barbecue. I found him slumped in a heap, sittin' by the barbecue. He hadn't done any of his chores. He was up on the roof one day and I couldn't get him to come down. The sheriff had to come like he was a cat or somethin'. Stella, I had to start to do every thing! I even asked him what he wanted for dinner and he couldn't identify what he liked to eat. He would even forget to shave or shower! And one day he left the burner on and, thank goodness, the teapot whistled. If I hadn't been in the other room, the house probably would have burned down," her mother ranted, the pitch of her voice rising. "There he was, Stella, sitting on the stool, ignoring the sound. He's suffering from short-term memory loss. Sometimes he doesn't recognize me nor is he able to distinguish any common items."

Stella switched the phone to her other ear. Her mother was a stoic woman, but she thought she heard the beginning of crying. Her mom needed a good hug and much more at a time like this.

"Momma, I hate to not be able to soothe your worries because I'm actually going to add to them. I feel terrible for telling you that I had to have a lumpectomy for a lump in my breast. They removed the cancer and were able to keep my breast intact. The margins were clean. I was one of the lucky ones." Her hand instinctively went to the site of the incision. "I have to rest a lot."

"How can I come to you now, honey? I have my hands full with your father." Her mother's voice went up another octave. "Are you okay, eh? Did Stuart stay with you during the surgery?"

"You don't have to worry about that. I always have support." She thought about the lie she had just told. But weren't her friends rallying around her, especially Cassandra?

"You betcha. You'll have me, too, in your heart. I'll be thinkin' of you every day, Stella." Her mother tried to gulp back her tears.

When she hung up the phone, she felt like she had been through the dishwasher with the dishes. She was dry one moment and dripping wet the next, fully drained.

This disease wasn't just about her breast. It affected her family, her loved ones, her friends, and all the people who cared about Stella. Her body would never be a perfect model body after they gave her the lumpectomy. Could she learn to love her body again? Stuart wasn't enjoying sex with her that much anyway. How would he react when he finally saw her naked? And would her libido ever return? Right now she felt like a fifty-year-old menopausal woman. Her fingers subconsciously ran through her silky locks. She would beat this awful disease, but she would have to deal with life after cancer too. And now her father! What could she do about him when she had herself to deal with?

UP THE LAZY RIVER

Harmony Cove sits on the banks of the meandering Wabash River, separating Illinois and Indiana. It was a good place for Steven to end up. This small town, located just a few miles from the interstate, opened up a friendly world for Steven's business. No prescription for his blues could work as strongly as the smell of corn in the open fields and the endless acres of soybeans. The townspeople were not a suspicious sort and they would never have heard of or read about Steven's rape charges. That was a thing of the past. Even in their eccentric styles, they were happy to participate in a spa-like environment, and he would find new clients every day who were willing to scoot over to his office on their bikes or the occasional golf cart. The town bandstand was busy every weekend with local kids who had gotten bands together out of sheer boredom. Sometimes bigger and more well-known bands would be out there on a Saturday night attracting the crowds.

Ice cream and refreshment stands sprung up like daisies. There were retail shops and eateries. All spring, summer, and even fall, you could find the townspeople milling about—friendly, courteous, and welcoming. There was a nostalgic feel to this new environment and Steven liked it more and more each day. The tranquil feel fit like a soft, buttery leather glove. He could stay here forever. He would just have to be careful with how he touched the women. And where would he score his coke? It was a small town, after all.

THE BOOK OF LOVE

Stella was feeling nauseous just thinking about the cancer. She needed to sit quietly. The doctor had said she would experience some minor inconvenience or discomfort. There would be short-term effects that usually disappeared in a short while after the surgery. She had been so happy to hear that she didn't need radiation therapy because the oncologist had said that would have given her skin sensitivity, fatigue, possible anemia, and perhaps even hair loss.

Stella was going to stay in control of her life. She was going to fight for a healthier life and maybe even a happier one. She curled up on the black leather lounge chair that she had bought for Stuart for one of his birthdays. He was never home enough anymore to even use the chair, but it would certainly suit her needs today. She reached for the book she had been reading, perched on the arm of the recliner. Unable to concentrate, she got up and pulled from the bookshelf a large book with photographs. As was her habit, she flipped through the pages just to feel their woody texture before she began the first word. A one-page, handwritten letter dropped to the floor. With some effort, she bent over to pick it up and began to read it instead of the guide.

Dear Stuart,

I know I work with you every day, but I must admit to you that it is becoming more and more uncomfortable for me to see you and touch you and have you, yet not be able to really have you. True, the sex is good and fun and even though it is dangerous for us to fool around in your office, in your private executive bathroom, or in the supply closet, or even on your desk, you go home to your wife every night.

I want you to come home with me. I have fallen in love with you and I know you have feelings for me, too. Your gentle touch tells me more than any words you could possibly speak, but I'm going to want to hear the words any girl would want to hear from her lover and that is that you are going to divorce your wife and get on with your life with me.

We can come to the office together every morning and we can go home together every night. I want to be with you forever and I know you want that too.

I'm sorry that I had to leave this letter for you, but hope that you will understand that it was easier for me to write these words rather than speak to you face-to-face. I would never think to tell your wife about us, but you must do that yourself.

> Your beloved,
> Cotton

This moment of discovery was the last straw. Stella felt that the world had finally closed in and she was looking through a scissor-cut slit, down a passage of secrets, as she began to close her eyes and grab for the arm of the chair. Dizziness added to her nausea as she sat down with such force that she had to grab where her incision was located as if to hold it in place. It may have been her breast that had been operated on, but her heart needed fixing.

Who the hell was Cotton and did Stuart have a nickname for every girl he met? Was the familiar form of Stella's proper name ever special? She had hated Stelli but happily accepted his tender and sweet name for her. Now it seemed he had a pet name for another. What else had he done for this girl?

If she could muster up the strength, she would go through every book on the shelf. Maybe there were more letters; maybe Stuart had written to this girl and had changed his mind about giving it to her. For fifteen minutes, Stella reached for the first book on the top shelf, then the next, then the next. So far, nothing. Her incision pulled as she stretched and she went to the pantry to retrieve a step ladder.

She shook the books with much vehemence and determination, hoping on one hand that she would not find any other incriminating evidence of his cheating, and on the other hand wanting as much proof as she could hold in two hands. Stella made coffee and brought it into the den with her. The spoon sat still in the cup. But she would not sit still for this. She would not weaken. She would wait for the night he got home for dinner and feed him the letter. She may be a naïve easy-going farm girl at heart, but she was about to become a ferocious beast.

The chair offered a respite and she welcomed it. Stella sat and wrapped her arms around her body to create warmth and tried to hold in her emotions. What would she do with a cheating husband? How could she face the cancer not only without Stuart's support but also without his love? She had fleetingly thought about a baby she might have with Stuart in the future. After all, her doctor had been emphatic about pregnancy not increasing the risk of a relapse. Now she was pretty sure that that wasn't going to be an option with Stuart.

There were less and less shelves to examine as her search came to a close. She made a mental note to tell the cleaning lady to dust the individual novels and volumes. Dust away these horrible findings, dust her beloved books that had dared to hold Stuart's secrets. There was one final book stuck on the very end, laying flat because of its sheer size. It was a table book entitled *Millennium Philadelphia: The Last Hundred Years* and it was heavy to hold and Stella could not shake its pages. She almost changed her mind but then grabbed it and sat back down.

How was Stella defined? Had her married life been a sham? She had trusted Stuart. He was handsome and debonair and his clients thought he was a great lawyer.

Her life had been punctuated by frills of every kind. A beautiful home in the suburbs, a shore house, a boat, cars, a luxurious life that many could only envy. But she had only begun to feel fulfilled when she became the mistress of her own domain. Owning the boutique had given her more than any lavish lifestyle could. She was challenged and excited and the life she had led as a model finally began to fade away.

The book weighed heavily on her lap and she flipped the first page. There it was! Balancing the tome, its clumsy weight on her lap, she grabbed the piece of paper. Stuart had purchased Cotton a condo in the city! The document was glaring at her, the bold words sneering, belittling.

That bastard! Maybe he would like this ream of paper reamed down his throat?

What truth was there in what her mom had always told her that men were good and she would always be happy? What foolhardy nonsense had this been? It surely didn't apply to her life. She had done Stuart good, and not harm. What had he done to her? No, all men were not good. It was a fantasy that her mother thought was true. Daddy was basically a good man and that was all she had ever known, but she had never been out in the real world where some men were good, but some were positively evil.

Stella fell asleep with the evidence clenched in her hands.

When she awoke, she rose to check the time. It was late afternoon and she had killed the entire day. But hadn't the doctor told her to rest?

She couldn't rest another moment. Her mind was racing and she went into the kitchen to try to keep herself occupied. The little green metal file held her mother's cherished recipes and maybe Stella could work with her hands and keep her mind off the situation for a while.

FOOD FOR THOUGHT

Bratwurst and red cabbage had been popular with her parents. In Minnesota there probably wasn't a family that didn't have those foods at their table regularly. Stella and her parents had sat down many a Sunday to enjoy their food in front of the television, watching the Vikings win their occasional game. They had rooted vigorously for their home team in spite of their many failures! They would even watch the Minnesota Twins when their season rolled around.

Potato croquettes had also been a favorite when she was a little girl and it was starting to feel like comfort food again. It would warm her belly. She had certainly been delivered mixed messages throughout her life. First, her mom had made her feel cozy and warm and loved with the yummy foods she prepared for Stella as a child. Then, when Stella became a model, she was told to stay away from fattening foods. In fact, she had witnessed many models staying away from food entirely; what little they ate was regurgitated! But it could never be her modus operandi to ignore food. It was ingrained in her to eat comfort foods. Instead, exercise became her god. Whatever went in her mouth would be sweated away, and after all, she had been blessed with skinny genes.

She slipped the recipe out of the file and reached for a bowl. The recipe card read:

> Add 2 tablespoons of milk, salt, ½ teaspoon of chopped green onion, 2 beaten egg yolks, and 3 tablespoons of all-purpose flour to 4 cups mashed potatoes. Chill and then shape using an ice cream scoop. Use 1 beaten egg to dip croquettes in and then roll through sifted dried breadcrumbs. Fry each croquette in shallow oil until brown on all sides. Don't overcrowd the pan!
>
> Oh, and honey, you can add cheddar cheese to the mix, if you like.

She smiled at her mother's extra notes. It brought her home to her mom's kitchen once again.

SPLITTING THEM UP

Margaret Crane Johnson Milhall March was turning sixty and she reflected on her life and her many husbands. They had all been bums as far as she was concerned. The first one, the father of her triplets, went along with keeping two of the boys and having the third given away. It was just too expensive to keep all three. He hedged about the second one, but she thought it would be harder for her if she kept one with no buddy for the other boy to pal around with. She really hadn't wanted any of them and keeping even two boys was exhausting. She had been proud that she didn't give up all of them. Steven and Stuart were cute kids and Seth was sweet, too. But he had to go. He was six months old before they decided to give him up. Seth had to have his bowed leg straightened and he had a hearing problem that had to be operated on. They just didn't have the funds to fix the kid. When the arrangement took place for him to go to another family, it was decided to keep his name because he was no longer an infant. Margaret laughed to herself. Poor kid had to deal with the name Seth all his life. In her mind, the names of the babies had to start with the same letter. She ran out of ideas after Stuart, Steven, and Seth. Good thing there weren't four of them! The name Seth would make him sound like he had a lisp all his life! And she knew in her heart that if the other two had anything medically wrong with them, they would have been gone, too. She had almost been nonchalant about giving Seth away, but she had to do what she had to do.

She pulled the trashcan to the curb and thought about how Seth had been given away, discarded like a piece of trash. She clutched her chest in memory of that decision. It hadn't been easy with the other two either. They were always fighting, boys being boys. But they had gone to college, having saved their money from their paper routes and their dog walking and babysitting jobs as well as other various moneymaking activities. Financial aid had helped tremendously too. On a rare occasion in their grownup lives, they had managed to call their mother. They hadn't been too grateful for all of her sacrifices. Didn't she wipe their runny noses? Hadn't she stuck a birthday candle in their store-bought cake when their occasion rolled around each year?

When she and her then husband brought the three babies home from the hospital, they knew their lives had changed forever. It felt like they were living on another planet. Multiple births might be more and more common, but when they're born to common people, things just ain't gonna work out!

The challenges were clearly difficult—medical, logistical, financial, and emotional. She hadn't done a thing to deserve triplets except to have sex. This was God playing a joke on them. You needed a lifestyle to have three babies. Sure, they had a roof over their head, but they struggled for every penny. It was a tug of war every month as to where to put the little they had. They got fed and then there wasn't much left for diapers, baby clothes, and formula. Sometimes it had been hard to keep the electric bills paid.

Half the time, her husband and she fought about who would get up in the middle of the night. Did he think she could handle three of them? She only had two breasts! Neatness was thrown to the wind. The house looked like a pigsty. Did he think she could cook, clean, and look after these kids? He stayed away as much as possible to avoid helping her. He enjoyed being there when he helped make those babies, but he'd rather hang with his friends after work than hang laundry and help with three babies. Three babies! Where were the rewards for having three kids? There wasn't anyone knocking at their door with cash prizes. No one was particularly fascinated with triplets. They weren't hitting the lottery. Maybe if she had taken fertility drugs, there would have been several babies and that could have brought them real attention.

She walked into her shabby house, slammed the front door, and put her feet up on the ottoman as she thought about the early years with three boys. And then there were two. There were plenty of times she wanted to pare them down to one kid. Hell, give them all away? But, she kept Stuart and Steven and as hard as it had been, she should have had a freaking medal for not giving them away, too. She had done the best she could. Hadn't she?

No, she could never recruit extra help. Her husband went off to work leaving her with the mess. Her parents were dead and she didn't have any support system. What was she supposed to do?

Margaret had trouble telling them apart. She smiled at the memory. When they were first born, they looked exactly alike. She was never bothered by the fact that she couldn't separate Steven from Stuart from Seth. Getting rid of one of them made it a little easier, but the two who remained still looked like the same baby.

She played with the TV remote in her hand while she thought about the time she had painted one toenail of each boy a different color in order to figure them out. It had been ingenious! When Stuart and Steven had become older, she wanted to dress them the same so other people would say "Ooh" and "Aah," but she wanted to keep up the color-coding of their toenails. As they grew past the toddler stage, those boys wouldn't hear of dressing alike or letting their mother come near them with polish.

Baby blues had hit her hard. It took its toll on her first marriage and she had had to go at it alone until she snared the second husband. Luckily, the kids' social skills had developed well and they were able to charm their stepfather when she married again. She shoved her glasses back on the bridge of her nose. Those little monkeys had made it seem easy when Man Number Two came courting. He truly believed it would be easy to keep them in control. Between the two of them, they played every trick in the book on him until he realized his stupidity at marrying her. Goodbye, Number Two.

They weren't too thrilled with her lifestyle and her many husbands, but after all, she was their mother. Where had that third boy finally ended up? It had been years. Their old neighbor, Christine, had taken Seth. She knew somebody who knew somebody who would give the kid a good home. There wasn't any need for going through legal channels, was there?

ERADICATING THE PAIN FROM HER BREAST AND HEART

Stella felt like she was on a merry-go-round of daily life, what with trying to take care of the house, looking after her boutique, and going to doctor appointments. Luckily she could compartmentalize everything in her brain just like her chest of drawers in her bedroom. She could separate the sad, the funny, and the happy moments in her life just like a sack of laundry. She could pull out a pile of love when she felt it and a load of hate and anger when she needed to wear those feelings. Stuart was causing a flood of emotions, as if a pipe had burst in her brain running all the colors together—blue for sadness, red for hot anger, and yellow for her happy color, like the sun, which wasn't appearing often enough these days.

She reached for her Prada Candy perfume and dabbed behind her ears as if that would seal shut the lid of her brain.

The bedroom door closed behind her softly and she took the stairs gingerly. The house was filled with things and not much else—no babies, no attentive husband, only a sweet cat who helped to keep her sane. The keys lay on the table in the foyer and she grabbed them and headed for the car. She would drive to do her errands, even if it were too soon.

THE DISCOVERY OF DECEPTION

When Harry Langhorne was sent from the IRS to audit the firm of Borders, Crane, and Yelds, he thought it would be an easy job. *Just take each day to look at the numbers, impart a little technical knowledge, teach them sustainable cost reduction and effective payable and receivable management, analyze costs, stamp his approval and go back to his cubbyhole proud of another job well done.* He never dreamt that he would be solving a mystery that had widened like the spreadsheets before him.

He had called his boss and told him that this was going to take longer than he thought. It required forensic accounting suitable for legal review. It would offer the highest level of assurance and, in Harry's independent professional judgment, would probably deliver a finding as to accounts, inventories, etc. that would be of such quality sustainable for legal proceedings. He was interpreting these evidences as very fishy and although that wasn't a scientific term, his boss understood all too well what was going on.

The discovery of deception required Harry to do an explanatory analysis. He was very focused on the falsifications and manipulations of accounts or inventories of the firm. He was beginning to feel a sense of importance. It was exhilarating to feel like he was onto something big and that the end result would be because he, Harry Langhorne, was brilliant and indispensable. The IRS would make him a star employee, perhaps even promote him and give him a bonus. He was playing an important preemptive role, detecting and interpreting the evidence of an abnormal and fraudulent accounting system. Someone in executive management would have to pay dearly for these improprieties. He was discovering all kinds of false entries like reserves for capital investments such as new computers and repairs. After some good old detective work, he didn't find one new computer and repairs to the current ones were minimal. He was starting to feel taller and taller and more important.

Perhaps the phones could be tapped in the offices of the partners? That would be a good place to start. He would check the legality of that and get the ball rolling. He rattled the pencils perched in a coffee mug and thought to himself, *I will rattle this cage!*

Yes, Mr. Langhorne would get major respect! He would show probable cause of unlawful activity and obtain a court order. Usually, the court order limits the surveillance to thirty days, but he could easily monitor these guys for that period. Something was bound to show up. Devious people who were involved in controversial activities deserved to be spied on. Maybe he wouldn't stop there. He could have their offices bugged, in addition to their phone lines. Getting permission wouldn't be easy, but with the IRS anything was possible.

What's this? Inflated prices for office space and inflated salaries for administrative services? A fake employee and a no-show job listed in order to qualify for medical benefits and a pension? What the hell was going on here? The value of a client's assets was underreported by a huge sum so he could qualify for a Medicaid-funded nursing home bed, ensuring the money would remain in the culprit's hands and not be paid to the government.

It was beginning to appear that someone in this law firm had misapplied or misappropriated several thousand dollars at the very least. Some greedy little lawyer was very busy milking the very place that lined his pockets. Harry had interviewed some of the employees who had supposedly received salary increases and the reaction was unanimous. They hadn't gotten a raise in a year and a half. How had the culprit put in for these employees to get raises and then pocket the money himself? He would dig through every inch of documentation until he unearthed the information he needed to get this person a lengthy jail sentence.

There were some very complex estate plans. Here was the name of a client who he had checked on yesterday and a family member answered the phone, only to tell him that the client was deceased. Why was he still being billed for services rendered?

Harry would try the number of the next client. The file stated that the client's banking, commodities, stocks, bonds, and mutual funds were being managed by the firm. He dialed Mr. Sult.

Someone picked up on the fourth ring just as he was getting ready to hang up the phone.

"Hello?" It sounded like the voice of an elderly man.

"Is this Mr. Sult?" Harry tried to sound even-toned so as not to alarm the gentleman.

"You got Mr. Sult. Who is this?" His raspy voice was practically a whisper.

"This is the accountant for the firm of Borders, Crane, and Yelts and I just need to verify which lawyer you are using," he questioned matter-of-factly.

When he placed the phone on the receiver, he smiled to himself. *This will make it easy for me to place the wiretap in the right office.*

ALL SQUASH LOOKS ALIKE OR IS IT JUST STUART?

When Stuart entered the supermarket, he was steamed, like the freshly cooked broccoli he had on his dinner plate last night. Cotton wanted to make a candlelight dinner for him and he had to come up with yet another excuse not to be home with Stelli. He pushed the cart a little bit harder down the aisle, thinking he never had been inside a food market for Stelli. Why was he here for Cotton? He was finding it harder and harder to be creative with excuses, but something always compelled him in the direction of Cotton. In the beginning, she had been a new conquest. Stelli was busy with her boutique and inconveniently tied up with her medical issues. When he bought Cotton the condo, he was thinking how suitable it would be for his own personal comfort and needs. After all, he was footing the bill, so he would pull the strings.

Until she annoyingly decided it was her home and she would control a few things, like him having dinner with her on certain nights. She would have liked it if he came for dinner every night and spent the night with her too. She was getting so damned demanding. Would it turn out that all women were the same? God, he hoped not!

They had been wrapping up a project and calling it a day when she said she expected him for dinner and would he please pick up an acorn squash that she could prepare?

What the heck did an acorn squash look like? He hadn't been inside a food market in eons. Stelli did all the shopping and she had never even asked him to pick up anything. For an ex-model, she was less of a demanding diva than Cotton, who had a very ordinary job and it was thanks to him anyway that she even had it. The farm girl in Stelli had worked well for him.

He squeezed a few melons and laughed to himself as he likened it to Cotton's breasts. It was busy in the market. Most people seemed to shop after work or on the weekends and the aisles were crowded with carts being pushed left and right. A pretty blond walked down his aisle and he purposely knocked his cart against hers. Oh, he loved blonds! *Let's face it, I love blonds, brunettes, redheads, any head!* She looked up at him and smiled. It would be easy for him to shamelessly flirt with her and maybe even get her to have a cup of coffee with him. But didn't he have enough troubles juggling the women he already had? He forced himself to look away.

When he finally found the squash section, he reached for one at the same time as another man. Stuart looked up to say, "Be my guest. You first."

"His eyes met the man's eyes, which were identical to Stuart's. "What the hell? Steven?"

"My name is Seth. Who are you and why do you look exactly like me?"

They both threw the squash back in the bin and stood facing each other like warriors.

Stuart spoke first. "I think we need to talk."

He canceled dinner with Cotton. She had screamed into the phone until he had a headache. He kept looking over at this obvious offspring of his mother and chose coffee with this complete stranger who was his mirror image. Was this some sort of joke? Steven had been trying to get a hold of him for a long time. Was this his way of getting his attention?

"Where were you born? Where did you go to school? Who are your mother and father?" Stuart rattled off the questions like he was in a courtroom, giving this unfamiliar person no time to respond.

He laughed. It sounded like himself. Deep, guttural guffaws. He spoke. It sounded like his voice. Again, deep, throaty words. He stretched out in the chair the same way Stuart did.

"Hold on with your questions. Let me try to answer them one at a time!" He was being short with him, the same way that Stuart was always cutting to the chase.

He paused as if he was thinking that he wouldn't answer the questions.

"Listen. I was given up for adoption. I had very loving parents who raised me. I never knew I had a twin brother, but I can tell you," and he hesitated again, "that somehow a piece of me has been missing all these years. It's like someone waved a magic wand and put you in that store at the same time as me." He took a long sip of coffee and pulled a piece of donut and shoved it in his mouth as if to buy time before he spoke again.

Stuart did the same thing. He popped the piece of jelly donut into his pie-hole as if to shut himself up. This was going to be his dinner and a very interesting one at that.

He continued. "I only just moved here recently for a job. I settled in and I've come to like the area very much. My wife and kids are happy, so I'm happy, too. Unfortunately, I was laid off pretty quickly," he said sadly, brushing over any conversation that might take place. "But I never expected a twin brother! This is a Philadelphia perk I could never have bargained for!" He was getting excited and his voice went up an octave.

Stuart continued to stare at him. He was surely on a planet of look-alikes. He lingered over his words as if they were as tasty as the donut. The waitress came over and filled their cups again, remarking that no two cups of coffee were ever the same because there were so many different types, but that the two of them must be filled with the same sugar and cream!

He added a packet of sugar and another container of cream at the same time this strange but familiar person did. He was identical; his gestures were identical; he waited impatiently for Stuart to speak.

"You aren't a twin."

"The hell I'm not. Look at yourself; then look at me."

"No. I don't mean that. You're a triplet."

Seth turned whiter than the cream in his coffee.

MIRROR, MIRROR ON THE WALL

The industry had made Stella glamorous and polished and she wasn't going to let a little cancer cramp her style. She stood in front of the mirror and examined the breasts that were giving her so much trouble. Ductal carcinoma in situ (DCIS) was the doctor's diagnosis. A lumpectomy. She thought about a mastectomy and when the doctor told her this was the most common type of non-invasive breast cancer, she opted for the invasion of the surgeon's hands. She didn't want to lose her perfect breasts, and the decision had been so difficult. The risk of recurrence after a lumpectomy and possible chemotherapy or radiation therapy was fifteen percent. She had decided that at this young age, she would make the choice to keep her breasts. Approximately sixty thousand cases of DCIS were diagnosed each year in the United States. She just didn't understand why, in her twenties, she became one of them.

Stella wiped the mirror with her sleeve as if she could take away all these decisions. The only humor she could find in all of her medical woes was the day she had gone to the gynecologist for an internal and a Pap smear. The doctor had smiled at her and said, "Stella, your cervix is adorable. It is the size of a walnut." They had laughed together over the comment and made an awkward situation so much more comfortable. Her doctor had been human and warm and cared not only about her body parts but also her mental health. Laughter was indeed the best medicine and she had actually left the office with a smile on her face.

The walk-in closet was filled with up-to-date clothes. She just wasn't an ex-model but also a high-end boutique owner too. She had to project an image and she might as well keep up the appearance of glamour no matter what she was doing. For even the most mundane errands, she would always look her best. You never knew whom you would run into.

Stella slithered into a tight black skirt with sequins. A little glitz would cheer her up. A black cashmere sweater set and a pair of stilettos finished off the look. The mirror looked back at her and she looked pretty good!

On her makeup table were the pearl earrings she had gotten from Stuart for her twenty-fifth birthday and she poked the posts through her pierced ears, added a little more blush for color, grabbed her purse, and headed for the door.

TRIPLE TROUBLE

Stuart needed a little recreation to clear his mind. After the encounter with Seth, he felt dizzy. He knew he should have been with Stelli (or Cotton), but this was more important. He had to shake the cobwebs from his brain. He put the key in the ignition and headed for the casino. He drove his beautiful, new car out onto the expressway and fell into place with all of the other cars rushing to their destinations. His car could find its way to the shore and the casinos without anyone behind the wheel! His life was getting so complicated. What had he done to himself? And now, he runs into a triplet? What had his mom done? She was always pushing Steven and Stuart together. Why had she pulled Seth apart from them?

Maybe he should play three card poker because surely the number three had major significance.

COLLECT UNEMPLOYMENT PLUS TWO BROTHERS

He opened his mail and there was his faithful unemployment check. Seth had been trying weekly to get a job ever since he lost his teaching position. He had moved to the Philadelphia area for better opportunities and there was absolutely nothing available. He would just have to stick it out until something came along. His wife and kids would struggle, but if the checks continued, he could manage to get by. He had been told that there was a drop in applications for unemployment and it signaled that hiring was strong enough to reduce the unemployment rate. Still, he was smart enough to know that the job market had a long way to go before it recovered from the damage inflicted by the Great Recession, which wiped out 6.7 million jobs. Some of the teachers whom he had briefly known were just about giving up hope of getting a job in education.

Seth would try to hang in there. Meanwhile, he was excited to tell his wife about Stuart and the other identical brother. The three brothers would have to meet up one day soon. His heart had raced from the moment he laid eyes on Stuart. There was a whole back-story and there were three look-alikes in this drama. The feeling of excitement overcame him. Maybe his life would change for the better. He had asked Stuart for Steven's phone number and he had told him he would look for it. He was excited to call him and somehow meet up. There were all kinds of opportunities in front of him, one being a family of triplets. He got in his car and drove to the bank.

OLD MEMORIES; NEW START

Steven was agitated. His brother was harder to get a hold of than the president. When he dialed Stuart's cell number, that annoying voice came on and told him to leave a message. He had a client in a few minutes, so he took a coffee break. He ripped the packet of sugar (nothing unnatural for him) and dumped it into the cup, along with a shot of cream. He stretched out on the old couch he had in his office.

There were good memories of the brothers, too. When they played in Little League, Stuart and Steven were always bumping bodies with great pride when they hit a home run and even hugged when they won a championship. They didn't really have a bond like most brothers and were hypercompetitive, but they put it to occasional good use. The competition worked in their favor when they played on the same team and tried to outshine each other. It worked to the benefit of the team. It reared its ugly head when they took tests, did homework, or jumped into the dating pool! They processed most information the same way, but did everything they could to make sure they were different. Their grades were mostly the same (their test results were similar) but the girls they chased after quickly figured out their game. One would hit on a girl and the other would show up for the date. If Steven liked a girl, Stuart always tried to win her over. The first sip of coffee to hit his lips was hot and he put the cup down to cool.

The front door swung open and brought him out of his reverie. His next client had arrived. They were few and far between and he had to cater to the ones who came to him. He had been so sure business would boom. The coffee never had a chance to cool down for him to drink. He rose to meet the woman who had the next appointment.

THE NAIL IN THE COFFIN

Langhorne had the tap in place. He had jumped through hoops and had to pull out all the stops with everyone he knew in order to get it done, but he had prevailed. It was the last nail in Mr. Stuart Crane's coffin. He had devised on-book schemes, drew illicit funds from clients' bank accounts, and made false records on the books for consulting fees and commissions. Payments were made to fictitious employees. There were kickbacks and overbilling schemes. In a fictitious payable scheme, a payable was created for a debt that was not owed. Through the establishment of fictitious vendors, payments were made to entities or individuals that did not exist. It was a clever method of hiding assets. But this fraud examiner was too smart for Mr. Crane. He analyzed the cash receipt and disbursement journals. His fingers danced on the evidence. He found ledger accounts with unusual activity. He even found a payment for design fees. Why would a law firm be engaged in a business that would not normally require such services? How did he ever think he would get away with this? And why would a partner in a law firm have to resort to this? Harry absentmindedly swept a piece of dust off of the desk he was using. Even housekeeping was questionable. He wasn't going to sweep the dirt under the table. He would dig it up, examine every grain, and expose it. He would have to talk to the senior partner and use him as an inside witness.

Crane was obviously sleeping with his secretary. She was in and out of his office more often than a dentist working on his mouth. Maybe she would talk.

He laughed to himself. Crime might pay, but the cash flow would be brief. A cost control specialist like him would make sure this review changed things for the better. He would schedule an appointment with Clive Borders as soon as the phone tap data came in. Audits weren't supposed to be confrontational, but he suspected his findings would create that atmosphere.

ANOTHER COKE, PLEASE

The car was parked near the casino entrance and he was in a hurry to get back to the office and do some work. Stuart handed the ticket to the valet.

The car was cold and so were the tables, signaling a huge loss for the day. He had been coming to this casino for years. Relationships had been developed. It never bothered him that even when he wasn't using the shore house, he would drive the distance to the shore. Well, his relationships at the casino weren't so loving at the moment. No one was reaching out with money to give to him. Stuart would have to figure out some other angle to obtain quick cash.

He glanced at his watch for the third time. He needed another hit and then he should get back to work. He was experiencing a variety of adverse effects on his body from the cocaine abuse. It was dilating his pupils and making his heart race. Or was it the illicit activity he was engaged in? Stuart was getting more and more headaches and he was suffering from abdominal pain. He had lost his appetite too. He had to be careful.

Regular snorting was causing a loss of smell. The perfume that Cotton wore had always titillated him, but not anymore. She had no appealing or unappealing aroma. She was beginning to annoy him too. She thought if he had bought her the condo, he was hers one hundred percent. Well, he was neglecting Stelli and he also had to be careful about that. Crap, he didn't want to contract HIV, or some other blood-borne or sexually transmitted disease. He had cheated on Stelli with Cotton, but he had also cheated on Cotton with plenty of other women.

He reached for the dashboard and put on some heat. He put the car in gear and took off down the casino drive to the exit.

MALIGNANCIES OF HER LIFE

She waited for the oncologist to enter the room. The nurse knocked and entered to take her blood pressure and temperature and measure her oxygen level. The cancer cells that had eaten at her breast like some alien baby had been cut out. When the doctor entered, he was intent on giving Stella full information as though he were a school librarian.

Stella tried to absorb all the facts. The doctor was so technical. She waited for him to leave the room so she could get dressed, but she closed her eyes for a moment and began to drift to thoughts of the other cancer in her life.

How would she confront Stuart about her discovery? He had a lot of explaining to do. Who was this woman named Cotton? (What a ridiculous name!) Was she a hooker or a pole dancer with a name like that? Stuart had never even mentioned a secretary's name. It had always been some clerical worker who helped out the partners. She always thought they had been too cheap to hire a permanent secretary. Could she have been so stupid?

Her doctor had said to try to live as normal a life as possible while she was recovering from this invasion in her body. What was normal? Her normal was abnormal—a husband who cheats on her, who never pays attention to her, who didn't seem to care about this major intrusion in her life. This cancer was an intruder, robbing her of her health and vitality. If it hadn't been for her friends, neighbors, and employees, she would not have had a support system. Stella pictured in her mind a long artery snaking its way between their home and his office, a valve blocked by a thick veil of bacteria stopping the flow of her husband's love.

She was determined to get strong and healthy. She was young and she would fight her problems like the gladiator she was. Her poor mom was working like a horse on the farm now that her father was ill. She was fostering the growth of the vegetables on their land. Stella was psychologically and surgically stopping the growth of cancer cells.

She pulled her sweater over her head.

THE DISCLOSURE

When Harry Langhorne finally asked to hold a meeting with the senior partner, Clive Borders was relieved that the IRS agent's work was done. He had hung around the office far too long and it was just supposed to be a simple audit. The guy looked like a nerd and must have thought like a nerd; otherwise, he wouldn't have been assigned the task. His mind should have been sharp enough to complete the formal examination and verification of the firm's financial accounts in a short period of time. What the heck was taking him so long? The knock on the door brought him to his feet.

"Have a seat, Mr. Langhorne," Clive said impatiently. "This has taken a long time."

"Mr. Borders, I think you should have a seat for what I'm about to tell you."

The meeting lasted two hours. Harry went over every fine detail, including the phone conversations he had pulled from the wiretaps in Stuart Crane's office.

"He's a crafty sort, your partner." Harry chuckled to diffuse the situation. "Crane's been embezzling from the firm for a long time and we took the liberty of putting in place a wiretap to try to overhear any plots to commit fraud. His conversations, especially with vendors, have been very interesting, to say the least. I had to turn over every legal stone and pull the right strings to unearth your financial problems."

Borders sunk farther down into his chair, like a deflated balloon. His voice went up an octave. "I gave the son-of-a-bitch control of the finances. I had been doing it for years and I wanted him to oversee everything for a change. He's younger and sharper, or so I thought. He's not sharp enough to escape your scrutiny and I'm grateful that you discovered all of this before years of building this firm came tumbling down. I thought he was a good man to bring in as my partner. Shows you how little I know about people." He shoved the papers in front of him to express his anger.

Langhorne closed his file and said, "Don't be too hard on yourself, Mr. Borders. The man is sly, clever, and resourceful. He didn't expect to be up against a worthy opponent like myself, if you don't mind me saying!" He leaned into Borders' desk as if to emphasize the weight of the situation.

Clive thought for a moment and decided he should hire a detective to follow Stuart around so they could get as much evidence against him as possible. "Let's nail him."

"Oh, that won't be necessary." Langhorne pushed away from the senior partner's desk. A ray of sunlight was shining through the window behind Mr. Borders and Harry broadly smiled, showing gleaming white teeth. "Let me shed light on the situation. After all, we are the IRS! I have enough on him to put him away for a very long time. I think it's the right moment to confront him. I'm sure he felt it was pretty easy to deceive all of you, but he didn't know he was up against Harry Langhorne!" He giggled nervously at his boastful assertion. "Auditors wouldn't necessarily catch fraud of this magnitude, but you got the best, if I may say so!" He felt bolder with every compliment he gave himself.

Clive was annoyed with himself. This little man turned out to be the one bright thing he did in this whole mess. He should have exercised more control as senior partner. He had given Stuart too much rein. It was time to tighten that leash and put him behind bars. "As soon as he comes in to the office, I'll be in his face. He'll be lucky if I'm not carrying a baseball bat to slug him with." Clive stood up and the meeting ended.

As Harry got up to head out of the office, he turned and faced Mr. Borders once again. "Wouldn't want to see you go to prison, too!" His nervous laugh escaped again.

THE MEAL TICKET

Cotton leaned against the closed door to Mr. Borders' office. She had heard every word. Her clenched fist was wrapped around the papers she had intended to bring Mr. Borders. When the two voices echoed from his office door, she couldn't help but stand there immersed in their conversation. A glance up and down the hall convinced her that no one was going to catch her standing at his door. If someone suddenly walked that hallway, she would grab the doorknob and appear to just be entering. In the meantime, she would hang on every word.

By the time Mr. Borders dismissed the accountant, Cotton was trembling. There went her meal ticket. No wonder Stuart could afford gifts for her and a nice little condo. He was stealing! She had to act as if she never heard a word and quickly ran to the top of the hall, turning to walk toward Mr. Borders' office as if for the first time, just as the accountant left. She would hand Mr. Borders the papers and go back to her desk and try to reach Stuart on his cell. She must warn him.

Stuart pulled over to the side of the road. He didn't want to be cited for talking on his cell while driving. His Bluetooth gave off static and he wanted to be clearheaded. He didn't need attention brought to him in any way, shape, or form. *Well, maybe in form! Cotton was in great form and some of the other women weren't too shabby looking, either!* He smiled to himself.

"Cotton? I'm heading to the office right now. Couldn't it wait?" He was annoyed with her trying to trail him. He put his flashers on and turned down the radio.

"No, Stuart! It cannot wait. I was just going in to Mr. Borders' office to deliver some papers when I overheard that little smarmy accountant talking to him about you. I stopped and put my ear to the door and hung on every word." She tried to slow her talking. "He discovered that you are embezzling! How could you, Stuart?" she cried. "I trusted you. The firm trusted you and now you could go to jail," she whined, her voice becoming high-pitched.

"What the hell are you talking about, Cotton?" his voice quivered. "You heard wrong!" he emphasized. "I haven't done anything. Why would I commit a crime against my own firm?" he asked indignantly. His fist pounded the steering wheel as if to stress the truth.

"I don't know, Stuart. You tell me. You'll have a lot of explaining to do when you show up to the office and if I were you, I'd figure out how to stay away." She hung up the phone.

Stuart sat there shaking. He had to clear his head. How could he explain all of this? Had they illegally wiretapped his office? They couldn't get away with that. It wouldn't be admissible. Had they spotted errors on his cleverly designed invoices? Those bastards! Clive brought him into the firm and he wasn't going to let him keep Stuart from his hard-earned profession. He wanted to kill them for bringing this trouble to him. How dare they question him! Damn, he needed a hit so badly. His car pulled away from the shoulder and nearly swiped a passing truck.

When he would arrive at the office, he would check thoroughly to see if they had wiretapped his phone. Wasn't there only a narrowly confined authority that could engage in this type of eavesdropping? Was there some sort of violation of his rights? He could try to turn the tables on them. Let those violators be imprisoned and given hefty fines. Sweat started to drip from his forehead. He pushed back his hair and pulled out a handkerchief to wipe his brow.

Was it legal to record his telephone calls? Or, would they come back with the statement that it was necessary to inspect the telephone system or to monitor the quality of service? Then, why wouldn't they inform him?

He couldn't return to the office. What was he thinking? They would be there waiting with a lot of questions. Should he consult an attorney even though he, himself, was one? Or should he hire a private investigator to get the goods on them? He had to think quickly.

PLAN A, B, C

It felt like the car was driving itself. He felt numb and he tried to put his brain in gear. Where could he go to think? Was Stelli home? He hoped not. He would drive home and formulate a plan.

The house was empty, just as he had suspected. He double locked the front door as if to keep the demons out and stormed into the den. The light from the computer looked like the white of an eye peering at him. He would not allow himself to get paranoid. The leather sofa looked cold and uninviting, but he plopped himself down and stretched out his long legs, putting his arms behind his head to act as a pillow. After a few minutes, he sat bolt upright.

Stuart's phone rang and when he heard the voice at the other end, he was shocked. "Hey, bro. What's up? You never return my calls and I've been wanting to talk to you for a long time." The air filled with background music.

"Turn it down, Steven," Stuart said a little too forcefully. "I've got a proposal for you that might be a lot of fun." He tried to sound playful.

"Remember when we were kids and we'd switch to mess with our dates' heads?"

"Yeah. That was fun. Wish we were still prankish like that. I've been missing the old days a little bit," he said wistfully.

Stuart had his opening. "What if I told you I need to get away from the office for a long vacation? I've been working my tail off and I haven't been able to take a break in so long and my senior partner would have my head if I took off for more than a few days. Our clients wouldn't appreciate that. They need to be wooed and wined and dined and how do you feel about pretending to be me for just a few weeks?" He pulled at the ear that wasn't attached to the phone as if to empty his brain and fly his crazy idea through the wires.

He climbed the stairs two at a time to the home office and turned on his other computer. He had to disappear. Was it enough to cover his ass with his twin brother, who seemed all too willing to cooperate, but might not show up? When they were kids, he never followed through with plans. His mind was always in a million directions. What about Seth? He had his number somewhere. He emptied his pockets and pulled out a handkerchief, a toothpick, and Seth's number. The cell phone was in his other pocket and he hesitantly dialed. His mind raced. Where had he put his stash?

"Yo, Seth? This is your look-alike brother, Stuart!" He tried to make his voice as light as possible.

Seth breathed deeply. "Nice to hear from you. We have a lot of catching up to do."

Stuart was impatient. He needed a hit and he needed it badly. "Yeah. Yeah. But right now I have a big favor to ask of you. You are out of work right now, correct?"

A MOUNTAIN TO CLIMB, OR TO HIDE AT A BEACH?

She pulled into the long driveway. The weather was getting warmer, but Stella felt chilled by the light breeze. Her arms pulled her red cardigan tighter around her, hugging her and giving her warmth. She went straight to the fireplace, making certain that the damper was open. Stella knelt to add the kindling to the grate and crumpled up the old newspaper. She struck a match to the big logs and stood to rub her hands together.

It was that time of year when she usually looked forward to the shore, but her boutique had to come first. Luckily, she had trustworthy employees, making it easy for her to come and go. Stuart certainly had an employee with no misgivings about stealing someone else's husband and playing house with him. He had hidden the fact that he had hired a secretary and she had been so naïve. Of course, he would have a secretary. It just never occurred to her to think about it one way or another. Was the farm girl still living inside her head? Was she that naïve? Had she been too focused on herself to think twice about it? She pulled back the curtain to let in the light, although, she had seen the "light" long ago.

The living room was filled with pictures from her modeling days. Above the fireplace was a portrait of her, seated on a settee, with a smiling face, looking as if she hadn't a care in the world. A diamond pendant's length embraced her cleavage and the artist had made it sparkle like her gleaming smile. How little she knew of what life was to bring her. There had been an innocence about her, but that was gone now. The artist had painted her portrait and she had become the picture of sophistication.

On the end table, by the green velvet sofa, perched pictures of her days on the farm, a solemn reminder of how happy her past had been. There was even a photo of Cat-a-Comb, her precious companion, who was always there for her.

The oriental carpet was in soft blues and greens and the two chairs facing the sofa were in striped chintz to pick up the colors in the rug.

Stella tenderly touched a picture of her mom and dad. Growing up on a farm with stoic parents who taught Stella how to be strong and fearless helped her succeed in the world away from Minnesota. How could she have thought farming was tough? Having a demanding husband, a business, and now battling a horrible disease, made her even more resilient. She could recover from anything thrown in her direction.

She headed for the kitchen to make some tea. Tea was always soothing.

She heard footsteps upstairs. The tea would wait.

"Stuart, are you home?" She tried to sound threatening. Was it an intruder? Was something else wrong with Stuart besides the laundry list of flaws she had already discovered? Why would he be home this soon and why would he be home at all? He usually found an excuse to be elsewhere.

He rounded the corner of the hall. Stella thought to herself, as she looked up at him, that he was as handsome as ever. His eyes sparkled with a hint of mischief and his hair was graying at his temples, even though he was still young. He was tall and slim and she thought to herself that was what she had fallen in love with—the façade, not the inside. How could she have been so shallow? How could she have so easily fallen for all the trappings that came with this life? It was at this moment that she longed for her peaceful childhood when there were no major decisions except when to feed the chickens.

She huffed a little from dashing up the steps. "Are you okay, Stuart?"

He followed her into the bedroom as she flopped herself onto the king-sized bed, fluffed up with the cushiest quilt and seven pillows piled high.

He stretched out next to her and wiggled himself close, touching her thigh with his. He put his right arm around her. Stella wanted to move away but was afraid.

This was the most intimate moment they had experienced in many months and she was afraid it would evaporate and the truth would explode her body into fine particles. He kissed her ear and started to cry. Huge sobs escaped from his throat into her ear, the sounds vibrating throughout her body.

"What's going on, Stuart? If this is about your mistress, I already know. I found the mortgage papers hidden away." She sat bolt upright, coming to her senses. She would not succumb to his hot, wet body, even though it had been so long. She was gaining strength in body and mind.

He pulled at her. "No!" She yelled with such force that she couldn't believe it was her own voice. "What have you done? Why would you spoil our marriage with your lies and infidelities?" She punched his arm until he pulled away.

Stuart knocked the tissue box over and reached down to the floor to grab it. He blew his nose. "It's much more than that, Stelli."

"And don't call me Stelli. I hate that name. My name is Stella! I want my old life back. You've made a mess of it. Who is she, this Cotton?" She picked at an imaginary piece of lint on the quilt as if to use it as a graphic for her silly name.

"No. You don't understand!" His voice went up, almost shrill. "I've cheated on you, I've cheated on Cotton, I've gambled away our life savings, I've embezzled from the firm, and I'm on drugs. There, I've said it all. It's out in the open and I'm sorry, I'm sorry."

He started to moan—deep guttural sounds, like a wounded animal.

She almost burst out laughing. Now there was a laundry list, dirtier than anything she could have imagined.

Stella slid off the bed and left the room.

Stuart thought about chasing after her, but he headed to the home office instead and typed into the search engine: "Safe places to live when running from the law."

He had to get away! His fingers danced around the computer keys, searching. The authorities might try to confiscate their computers, but he'd be long gone. Luckily, he had built up a cache of money offshore. He would grab that in order to live.

I'm so glad I got those brothers of mine to agree to show up at the firm. One of them would surely do it and if both suckers show up at the same time, I'll be out of town before the shit hits the fan. They can buy me the time I need.

Aruba. Their legal system was so messed up. Did they have an extradition treaty? Didn't that kid get away with murdering that young woman from the States? Didn't that guy with the awful toupee get away with murdering his girlfriend? Yes, that was the place to be. Any investigation that would take place in Stuart's name would take forever. They wouldn't throw him back to the wolves in the United States.

Beautiful Aruba. Divi-divi trees dotted the landscape, distinctive by their wind-sculpted shape, and pristine white beaches and blue waters. The island attracted more than eight hundred thousand international visitors annually. Stuart scrolled down as if he were looking for a vacation retreat. He could get lost among them. Stuart would feel like he died and went to heaven. He could probably get his hands on all the drugs he wanted. He could consider suicide, but why would he destroy his life when he could continue to live the high life? Enough money was hidden away and he could live off of that for a very long time. The creditors may come knocking, but that door would be unhinged, with part of it open only to him. He had the gun to protect Stelli and himself, but he was not about to use it and blow away his chance at continuing to enjoy the finer things in life. He'd find another Cotton, another Stelli, without any trouble. There would always be a beauty waiting for him wherever he might end up.

He was feeling better already. He had gotten everything off his chest. He wanted a clean slate with Stelli before he ran. It made him feel better and he didn't give a damn if it made her feel worse. Sure, he would have liked to have sex with Stelli one more time, but that wasn't going to happen. He would order his airline ticket and get the hell out of there fast.

Stella never felt angrier. First, sexual infidelity, and now financial infidelity. The cup of tea was cold and she pushed it aside. That bastard had been keeping all kinds of secrets from her, sneaking around, doing all kinds of things to ruin their lives. Cat-a-Comb peaked around the corner of the chair and she called to him to come cuddle with her. With all these cloak and dagger dealings, she was happy her beautiful cat wasn't black.

That would be an omen she couldn't have faced. She grabbed him and hugged him as if he were her only ally. The oncologist had told her to try to reduce stress in her life. Oh, if only she could explain. She stroked his fur and finally decided to come out from under her safety net. She waited for Stuart to run down the steps and explain himself. There was no sound.

The liquor cabinet hadn't been opened in ages. Stuart was always out and Stella didn't drink very much. But today necessitated a drink. The doctor had also said that it wasn't wise to drink too much after what she had been through. Maybe it could lower her immune system even further. Cancer and vodka were probably a lethal combination. But, it couldn't be more lethal than the combination of Stuart and Stella. Well, one drink wasn't going to kill her. She poured straight vodka into two glasses and went to get the ice.

Each step was an effort, but she would climb up and confront him again. She wasn't going to let him get off so easily.

Stuart whipped around in his chair looking like the cat that swallowed the canary. He hit the screen saver and motioned to her to sit in the chair opposite him. She slammed down the second drink, almost shattering the glass.

"Stella, I didn't want it to end this way." He sounded contrite. "I never thought I would get in so deep. The gambling took hold and then everything just fell apart." He reached to touch her knee and she jerked away.

The room was starting to spin. "Thank goodness no checks have bounced, Stuart. You've made such a mess of things. Is your IRA gone? Are all of our personal funds gone?" She turned bright red with fury. "It was bad enough that you had your little torrid affair, but the debt you've incurred!" She started to raise her voice. "We're over, Stuart. I can't look at you another minute." The tears rolled down her face. "Money has always been your power and you've been playing this game too long. I hope you rot in hell!" The glass in her hand felt like a weapon. She wanted to kill him. At that moment, she hated him more than she had hated anyone in her entire life. The gripped glass left her hand like a hurling football and went straight for the computer screen.

As hard as it had been to walk those steps up to their home office, that was how easy it was for Stella to run down them. She grabbed her jacket and headed out the door for a walk.

Her mind raced. She would leave him. She would probably lose everything and she felt nauseous. When she returned to the house, she would place a call to a realtor. She had to get rid of their beautiful house and the boutique in which she had invested so much time. The neighbor's front gate afforded her support as she grabbed for one of the wrought iron spokes. She went from feeling chilled to sweating. Expensive cars dotted the driveways and Stella wondered if the men who lived in those houses had paid for the frills and perks of their lives with honestly earned money, or had they stolen to boost their incomes and maintain a rich lifestyle? When she had walked two blocks, she turned back. The short walk felt like a mile and as she passed the large houses on the street and the beautiful flowering dogwoods, elms, cucumber tree magnolias, and sweet birch, she thought of the ordinary life she once had. But she would recover from it all, especially the deep shame that her husband had plunged her into.

It had been phenomenal when Anne discovered her, a way out of her boring young life. She thought she wanted all the trappings, the good life. But what did she really want? Could peace only come with the simple life? Now, she longed for boring. Instead of folding sweaters and carrying on a charade of a life, she yearned to be riding the tractor alongside her father, plowing the fields, instead of cultivating a fancy lifestyle. One of her chores had been to turn the crank on the cream separator. She would turn it just right and her mom would always let her pour the rich cream on her cereal and mix it with the milk. They had even hatched their own chicks. Now, she would never have a baby with Stuart. It had been such fun to hunt down dried corncobs and dead wood sticks from the yard. Her father had taught her not to complain because maintaining a happy heart in the face of adverse conditions was said to build character. It was nearly impossible to put on a happy face with her world collapsing around her, but she would try.

It might be fun to go back to her roots and lose herself in the chores of the house and the farm. She could feed the sows in the hog barn and watch the mice scurry in the corncrib. In spite of herself, Stella smiled at the memory of the sow who had just delivered her piglets and had charged Stella until she ran all the way back to the front porch, calling for Mama.

There were animals to feed and cows to milk and she could help Mama get the meal on the table. She could use her help with Dad's memory slipping away.

The chores would rain down upon her as if it were the strongest storm, helping her to forget. How could she stay in the Philadelphia area? She would be the laughing stock of her neighbors; people she had known in the fashion industry would shun her. No one would be interested in any kind of relationship with the wife of an embezzler.

Once she put a realtor in place, questions could be answered by phone and she could get out of town quickly. She would get a broker to sell her business. Papers could be signed and mailed back and forth. This was the least of her troubles.

WHEN IN DOUBT...

She couldn't go back to the house. The garage door was open and she slid into the driver's seat of her car. Stella hadn't been to church in years. Stuart wasn't interested in organized religion and although Stella had been raised a Catholic, she hadn't practiced her religion since the beginning of her modeling days. The neighborhood church was appealing to her now and she would head there for answers. There would be no praying for Stuart. He had to answer to God in his own way.

The word *catholic* meant "throughout the whole, universal." Whole what? Whole life? Whole married life? Whole career? She smiled to herself. Nothing in her life had been whole and she laughed at the idea of using the metaphor while she felt as if she were slipping into a different kind of hole, sliding deeper and deeper into oblivion. Her simple life had not lasted, her modeling career had not lasted, her marriage had not lasted. Nothing was whole.

The pool of water that everyone was baptized in greeted her at the door of the church. She dipped her hand in the water, made the sign of the cross, and attempted to renew promises that her parents had made for her when she was baptized. The reconciliation chapel was located in the baptismal area and the practice of confession arose from the need to reconcile Christians who had neglected or ignored their baptismal promises. She was certainly in that category.

She had practiced her faith when she lived in Minnesota; of course, she had no choice. Her parents were strict Catholics and regular churchgoers. She went along for the ride or she would have been punished.

Would a God, no matter what your religion and what God you believed in, let awful things happen to good people? Why was she being brought down along with Stuart? It was his bad behavior and he had to own it. She hadn't bought into it. Why would God put her through this? She had been so blessed in the beginning with riches of all kinds. Now, she felt as poor as the church mice running about.

Could she go back to modeling? She was on the old side of the age desired by the media. No agent would want her now. She wouldn't be able to keep her boutique. If she wouldn't be allowed to sell it, they would find a way to take it away from her and she'd never be able to recover her good name. If the authorities didn't take it from her, her name would still be tossed about like some beach ball carried away on an ocean wave. The rumors would fly and she would all of a sudden become poison in the fashion industry.

Wasn't she obligated to pay her husband's debts? Even if she could hold on to the boutique, there would be a million questions once the story hit the papers. When Stuart would be arrested, everyone would want to know the full sordid tale. She couldn't stand reliving it over and over again. The shore house, the main house, the boat—would all be taken back by the banks? Stuart had managed to lose everything. He even drove her to lose her faith.

Stella knelt at the pew. The church floor symbolized the foundation of faith. Her foundation had been rocked to its core. Would she ever be able to find God again? Would she be able to move back to Minnesota?

Could Stella find the peace she so badly craved? She had stepped into a raging tsunami of problems. It was time to save herself and come up for air. It was gut-wrenching. She felt a mix of shock and disgust. She had to remain calm. Stuart's admission of guilt to her may have made him feel better, but it deeply hurt her. He had found himself in a powerful position, with women throwing themselves at him. Stella, on the other hand, had remained devoted and faithful. The men who had hit on her (and there had been many) had been ignored. She was married and she would keep her promise to be faithful. The anger she felt surfaced like bile and she swallowed hard. The church bells rang out and brought her back from her deep thoughts. She looked at her watch. It was time to make a few calls.

She walked to the church parking lot and slid into the front seat of her car. She adjusted the mirror and caught her reflection in the sunlight. Wasn't it Picasso who had said that there were two types of women—goddesses and doormats? Hadn't she felt like a goddess when she had been discovered by Anne? When did she become Stuart's doormat? He had been so charismatic and immensely talented. She had been drawn to that. She had let him control her life and she felt a deep anger for having bent to his every whim. She was too taken up with their nouveau riche life to notice his narcissism, his egotistical manner, and his self-centeredness. She really was only a farm girl. Her life had always been under the control of others. First, her parents, then Anne, and finally Stuart. Oh, how people would laugh at her! You can take the girl away from the farm, but not the farm away from the girl. That adage was all too true.

She reached for the cell phone lying on the passenger seat. There were several texts and missed calls from Stuart. His voice squeaked like a little church mouse. He was more like a rat. He was leaving. He couldn't face the authorities. He was sorry for the mess he had made of their lives.

She hit delete.

"Cassandra?" She could hear the whine in her own voice. How she had wished she had a sibling to share everything with. She would have had a powerful bond with a sister or brother, unlike Stuart who didn't give a damn about his own twin. Cassandra had taken the place of a sister. She had been able to share everything with her. Their relationship could never change the fact that she missed having a sibling, but it was close and so were they.

"Stella? Are you okay? How are you feeling? Do you need me for anything?"

"I'm almost totally healed, Cassandra. It wasn't so awful after all. You've been so supportive of me and I couldn't be more grateful." She bent her head into the phone as if to tell her a secret.

"We're friends." Cassandra laughed. "That's what friends do!"

Stella cleared her throat, almost unable to get the words out. "I just want to vent. That's why I called. Things are a mess here." She grabbed for a tissue and dabbed at her eyes.

"Is it the boutique? Financial problems?"

"Yes and yes. Not that the boutique is failing. It's been doing pretty well, but Stuart has gotten himself into a heap of trouble and everything is going to be taken from us. And I'm afraid the shop has to go, too. I'll need to explain another time. I just wanted to let you know that I'm considering going back to Minnesota." She sighed. "I'll keep in touch wherever I end up."

Cassandra blew out a breath of air. "I knew he was trouble from the beginning. I'm so sorry for all of your problems, Stella. That bastard should be looking after you now that you have cancer. He shouldn't be adding to your woes. He's the disease eating away at you." She raised her voice.

Stella started the car. "I'm not going to let him do that to me. I will go and find peace where my life started; I will refuel, replenish, and rethink. In due time,

I will start over again," she stated as if she believed her own words.

"I'm there for you whenever you need a shoulder to cry on."

THE FLIGHT

The Philadelphia International Airport and the City of Philadelphia welcome you to the birthplace of our nation.

Stuart read the sign and grimaced. He would have to say goodbye to the City of Brotherly Love with its shopping, entertainment, nightlife, and unique variety of hotels and attractions. He had loved Philly and he had loved the shore. Now, he had screwed up big time and might never see either again. His fingers curled around the handle of his carry-on as he dragged it through the international concourse to his gate. He passed the food court and decided to come back for something to eat before the plane boarded. He had time to kill before the flight took off. Art exhibitions were on display everywhere and Stuart was too preoccupied to even notice them. The boarding pass was shoved into his back pocket and he had to start pushing away all ugly thoughts of his actions. Why had he been so greedy? Why had he let the gambling get to him like that? Why had he thrown everything away? He had kept a gun in the house for protection, but he couldn't travel with it. That was all he needed—to be stopped by security. He had thought about using the gun on himself, but he had displayed enough loathsomeness to Stelli. He would not display his guts too. He was too vital, anyway; he would enjoy his life, not destroy it. He shoved his sunglasses to the top of his head.

He had snorted some coke before he left for the airport. It would have to hold him until he got settled somewhere five hours away. The seat at the gate was hard and cold like his heart. He'd fly away to Aruba and melt his worries in the sun. And the minute he got heat from the authorities again, he would move on.

THE PERFORMANCE

Strike. Seth rolled the ball down the alley with such force. Why had he said yes to his newly found brother, Stuart? What a folly! The only reason he would even consider it was because he had been laid off from his job and he had time on his hands even though he was steadfastly looking for work. He would fill in for Stuart at his office until he returned and he'd make it fun. It could be like an acting gig and he could easily pretend to be his brother. He hadn't grown up with him, but their gestures seemed the same; their ideas and attitudes had to be the same, didn't they? After all, they were identical. He would go to his office and execute the best rendition of his brother. Another strike! He would score on both counts!

———⁓⁓∽⊙⊶⊙⊷⊙∽⁓⁓———

This was the last client of the day and Steven was glad the hours had passed so quickly. Stuart finally needed him and he would close the office for a week and sit in for his brother at his firm while he was away. It would be so cool to portray his brother. Steven felt important. It was true. Stuart did need him. After ignoring so many calls that he had made to him, it warmed his heart to finally have made contact and to cook up this little scheme together. It felt like old times. He threw the towels and sheets in the laundry bag, sterilized the massage table, shut out the lights, flipped to the closed side of the sign, and locked the door. On Monday, he would stroll into Stuart's office and play the role of his life.

GOD BLESS AMERICA, LAND OF THE FREE: GOD BLESS ME!

When she pulled into the garage, she had a sense of loneliness and despair. She could no longer wait for Stuart to walk in the door. He was gone. She would have to shake off her old life like dandruff, getting rid of the unattractive and telltale scurf. She had to go back into the house and face the music alone. But it had to wait. She let the car idle in the garage while she tried to think and then closed the garage door and shut the engine off. She felt like she could keep the engine running with the garage door slammed shut and she could die of carbon monoxide poisoning. But why should she give Stuart the pleasure of the final act? Let him suffer. Why should she kill herself in the name of what he had done? Stella closed her eyes. It was as if she had fallen down the black hole of a wishing well and all of her wishes had washed away. She had leaned too far into the well of wishes and she was drowning.

Where was God in all of this? Going to church had been a mistake. It had not restored her faith in God and the doubt was a very tough place to be. Wasn't it her faith that should keep it all together when facing life's challenges?

She opened and closed the ashtray. Back and forth. Back and forth.

This was a catastrophe. Stella would live through the cancer and she would get better and stronger. She was young and in time she would be back to that energetic place she had been. But this was too much to handle on top of managing the disease. How could she cope with both at the same time? She pushed away the disruptive thoughts and opened her eyes again, surveying the contents of the garage, which she would have to clean out.

Those distracting thoughts—would they be noticed by God? Could she sweep away her doubts before she slipped away? Stella was frightened. Didn't God care? Was he listening? Did he even exist?

Quiet desperation was building inside of her. She was ashamed that she wanted to walk away from her faith, as she would walk away from this life she had known.

The enemy of faith should be doubt, but the real enemy here was Stuart. He had destroyed their lives together. She didn't deserve to feel shut down. It was his fault; he had handed her a harsh reality. She felt bitter, like so many winters could be.

Once, when she was little, she had touched the hot stove and burned her hand. It had left an imprint on her and this, too, was a scalded image of failure.

No, she wouldn't let him destroy her. Transformation would wash away her fears. A metamorphosis would not only clear her head, but sweep away this former life.

How could she be worthwhile once again? Stella got out of the car with determination. She worked furiously to pack up the house and clean out her and Stuart's old life together. Dust flew everywhere. There would be no time to chastise the cleaning lady. A simple note taped to the door would have to serve as her termination. Stella thought about alerting the neighbors to her decision, but she wanted to get out as fast as possible. Perhaps she would attach her cell number to a piece of paper at the back door in case the authorities wanted to have a chat with her. She wasn't the one who would fear the truth. Let them have as much information as she possibly knew. There was Cotton; there were drugs… well, she'd tell them anything she knew. Her life could go into storage or the boxes could be thrown away, for all she cared. The necessities would be all she would bother with.

Stella continued to empty her closet and hoped she could bring most of it with her, although, where she was going there was no place for silk and chiffon. But how could she part with her beautiful collection of clothes? True, it was all part of this hideous old life, but to give away her beautiful things was like enduring a surgery all over again, cutting away another part of her. She had to force herself to ditch this shallow life she had participated in for far too long. Stella would go to her boutique and write the last of the checks for the employees and try to explain the loss of their jobs. It would be true to say her parents needed her. All other details could be left out. The real truth would turn to bitter herbs on her tongue.

She would return to her roots and once again feel the country earth beneath her feet. She would get up early, feed the farm animals, ride the tractor, and focus on her folks instead of herself. Maybe her father would recognize her and she could help him improve.

She dropped her doubts at the kitchen counter like a grocery bag filled with new and organic food. Yes, this could be a new beginning even if her life had already started there. She would go back and begin her rebirth.

LET THE GAMES BEGIN

What makes a good lawyer? Clive sat at his desk pondering the question. He always thought he was a good judge of people. Hadn't Stuart displayed the qualities he was looking for at the firm? The files were piled up in front of him. Could he open a file and concentrate on his work? He looked at his watch: 9:00 a.m.

It was Monday morning and Stuart was bound to come in at some point. Clive would have Cotton buzz him the moment he stepped off the elevator. He would confront him with the evidence and tell him to clean out his desk and get out. Stuart would hear from the authorities very soon.

Cotton was nervous. She would lose her condo and she would lose Stuart. What had she gotten herself into? *I'm an idiot for getting involved with him,* she thought to herself. Mr. Borders demanded that she buzz him the moment Stuart got off the elevator and she debated whether to feign illness and go home or stay and face the monster that had ruined everything. In the past, she had wished Stella dead so she could have him all to herself. When he had told her that Stella was suffering from breast cancer, she had to admit that she was happy. He would be all hers in body and mind. Why would he want a sick wife? Surely, he would have divorced her for Cotton. That had been then. Now, she wished *he* were dead. Her fingers danced across the computer keys with a vengeance.

Steven whistled as he parked his car. Since they obviously drove different cars, if anyone asked him questions, he would be prepared to say his car was in the shop. This was going to be fun. He waved to the guard as he thought Stuart would do every morning and took the elevator up to the seventh floor. Stuart had told him where his office was located and he would nonchalantly stroll to it as if he belonged. He straightened his striped tie and put his attorney face on.

The door glided open and he stepped into the firm's foyer.

Monday morning. Clive loved Mondays. He loved the sounds in the office: the clicking of the computer keys; the hum of the copier; the lawyers, paralegals, and assistants buzzing around; the phones ringing. The start of business as usual. However, he did not like the sound of the word *embezzlement*. The word rolled off his tongue like poison. Every morning, the mailman would greet him by tapping on the glass surrounding his office. A friendly wave would be offered at the same time every morning. Clive could count on the mail arriving promptly. Cotton had delivered it to him on this sunny Monday and he had immediately reached for the letter opener, a gold sword-like instrument knotted in a loop at the top.

The detectives would be questioning him, as well as Stuart. He could expect a subpoena from the Commonwealth of Pennsylvania for him to appear in court to testify against Stuart. The wheels were in motion. They had taken the necessary steps to protect themselves and ready the firm for Stuart's imminent departure. This lawyer was going to need a lawyer!

The buzzer sounded. It was Cotton.

"Mr. Borders!" Her voice was high-pitched, scared. "It's Stuart. I mean Mr. Crane. He has arrived."

Clive dashed to the foyer. "Stuart!" He raised his voice. Steven kept walking and then slowly turned. *Oh, yes*, he thought. *I'm Stuart this week. Better play the role of my life! But, who the hell was this?*

"Good morning. And how are you today?"

"Don't give me any of your bull, Stuart. We're on to you. You have one hour to empty your desk and clear your office." Clive was red in the face. "How much time do you think you'll serve in prison for embezzlement? Well, let me tell you. The authorities say it could be up to six years, then probation for probably ten years, not to mention paying this firm back double what you stole." He shook his finger in Steven's face.

The staff had started to gather to watch the persistent assault. Some of the staff would bask in the glare of Stuart's punishment. He was arrogant and a know-it-all. He was only getting what he deserved anyway. Hadn't they been ignored by this pompous ass? A sea of high heels and ties caused a current of curiosity.

Steven stood stock-still. A tic started to form in the corner of his eye to the rapid rhythm of this man's words. What the hell? He pulled at his tie, all of a sudden feeling like he was wearing a noose around his neck. His hand wiped at his nose like he was sawing firewood.

Did he say to start Tuesday? Seth thought to himself. Hadn't Stuart told him he had an all-day meeting on Monday and he should go in on Tuesday? He shook his head. All of a sudden he couldn't remember.

The lack of continuity in his life was causing him to be forgetful. When he was teaching, he would get up at the same time every day, follow the same routine, and teach. Then he would come home and write his plan for the next school day and sit down at the dinner table with his wife at exactly 6:00 p.m. Clock-work.

Now, he was filling his hours looking for a job, but when that didn't fill his entire day, he would bowl or go to the library, or create chores around the house. He lost track of time very easily.

No. Seth was sure Stuart had asked him to go in on Tuesday.

This was easy. Seth had dressed in a tie and jacket to teach school. He wanted the respect of his students and that was one way to command it. An attorney would look the same. He straightened his striped tie and checked the mirror one more time. His wife had left for her job. Thank goodness, one of them was working. He hadn't told her what he was doing for his brother. She would not have been happy. After all, he barely knew him! He told her he would be out all day searching for a position. Why, maybe the law firm wouldn't mind hiring Stuart's brother. Once Stuart returned, Seth could pretend he had never covered for him and he could apply for some kind of administrative position there.

"We have a problem, sir." Cotton's voice was shaky. "Security walked Stuart, I mean Mr. Crane, out yesterday. He just walked into the foyer as if nothing ever happened."

"Is this some sort of game you are playing, Stuart?" Clive thought he would have a heart attack. His heart started racing and his head started pounding. "I've had just about enough of you!" His face reddened in anger. He grabbed Seth by the fabric of his jacket and pulled him with all of his strength. "Get out of here! I thought you cleared your desk yesterday! What were you thinking to come back in today?"

Seth tried to clear his throat. The words wouldn't come out fast enough. He was just supposed to pretend he was Stuart for one lousy week and then go back to his normal life. Why weren't they happy to see him?

Clive slammed him against the closed elevator door. "Cotton! Get security fast!"

He found his voice and in barely a whisper said, "What have I done? You knew I went to a meeting yesterday!"

"A meeting? What are you talking about? I knew you lost your mind when you embezzled from us, but now you have clearly gone completely over the edge. You were here yesterday and security marched you out. Now, they are going to take action all over again. This will not go well when you are on trial. Now, get the hell out of here and stay out." Clive pulled at the tie around Seth's neck and he thought he would pass out. What had this newly discovered brother done to him?

ROOTS

She was torn. Now that she was focused on going home to Minnesota, she couldn't find a place for herself. Like a dog making circles to find his comfort zone, Stella tossed and turned in her lonely bed, devoid of Stuart's presence. The night seemed to go on forever, like a long and boring conversation, interrupted by few pauses, frequent sighs, and a scream catching in one's throat, trying to yell *stop. Stop.* She grabbed the pillow with the satin pillowcase, and placed it over her face hoping to turn off the nightmare that had become her life. The authorities had called to see where Stuart was. He was gone. Didn't they understand? He had run from the lives they had shared. She pressed the pillow harder into her face until she gasped for breath. She had been told that they had two more conspirators who looked exactly like him. What were they talking about? Three look-alikes? She knew Stuart had a twin, but a triplet? His secrets were layered like the tiers of a cake, hidden under spoiled icing.

In the morning, she would throw the linens in a box and pack the rest of her bathroom needs and meds into her suitcase. Next, she would find a jeweler and cash in all of her gold, presents that Stuart had given her throughout their marriage. She would never wear any of it again, never wanting to be reminded of happier times that were fake from the start. Even though she was more curious than Cat-a-Comb, she would not dare to hang around to see what stupid plan Stuart had hatched. The clock ticked. 2:00 a.m., 3:00 a.m. Stella glanced at it every hour. The morning could not come fast enough. She got out of bed in the middle of the night. The bathroom mirror stared back at her. She was still young, still beautiful. She was grateful that her hair wasn't going to fall out and grateful that she was going to be healthy again. Would she find the nerve to change her life, as she would her outfits? Or should she stay and rebuild her life? No, she would return to the farm even if it seemed her life was spinning backwards.

They just had to find Stuart. Triplets? A brother had shown up on Monday and a different brother had shown up at the firm on Tuesday. It was a ridiculous decoy Stuart had set up in order to get away. He must have known he had idiots for siblings in order to devise such a stupid plan. They had fallen for it and fallen for his charms just as she had, and once Stuart was arrested and brought back from wherever he was, the three of them would spend time in jail. The authorities were no fools, even if these three were. They had the brothers in custody. And they were out looking for Stuart.

If she could only find Cat-a-Comb! Where had he hidden himself? Stella searched his usual hiding places and lastly lay down beside the king-sized bed to search beneath it. There he was! But her night table drawer was wide open and wrappers from candy and the sedatives she kept there were torn open. The cat's tongue hung limply at the side of his mouth and he was breathing heavily. She would have to get him to the vet before they left on their journey cross-country. How would she explain a stoned cat? This was just another obstacle to her plan. She needed to get out of that house and fast.

Luckily, the vet had emptied Cat-a-Comb's stomach and he was no longer in a drugged stupor. He would be fine for travel. She put him in his cage to sleep off the remnants of his drug and sugar-filled escapade. The suitcases were locked in the trunk. Stella searched for her key and double locked the door as if to keep the creditors away forever. She fiddled with the knob back and forth to secure it, making certain it was locked. She didn't know if she was locking up the house or shutting out her emotions.

The GPS had been a great gift from Stuart. He had no idea when he gave it to her that it would carry her away from him. She set the GPS. Stella would find her way toward Cleveland, then to Chicago, cross into Wisconsin, and finally arrive in Minnesota. She would go on a different kind of adventure leading her home.

She drove at a safe pace and imagined a trail of breadcrumbs strewn from Philadelphia to her birthplace, as if to conjure up a fairy tale. A lightening bolt struck a jagged pose through the gray-blue sky and she pulled over to let the storm have its way. She put her hand outside the window, feeling the knife-like sheets of rain keeping her awake and alert. *Wherever Stuart was now,* she thought to herself, *I hope the bastard is struck by lightening.* Stella watched as hail-sized balls hit the windshield. She leaned her head against the headrest and let the rain wash the car and wash away her wicked thoughts. Cat-a-Comb meowed with all his strength, frightened of the sounds and sights of the sudden cloudburst.

Every so often, Stella reached back to feel the cat's breath on her hand. He had awakened with a start and although the drugs had worn off, he was meowing like a scared kitten. Each breath out was blowing away the life her pet had shared with them.

The storm blew over as quickly as it had arrived and other cars that had pulled over too began to turn onto the highway, their owners in a hurry to reach their destinations. By the time Stella reached the first stop along the journey, the cat would probably be more himself. And the farm would be so good for him. He could run freely, play with the animals, and follow her around all day.

She turned the radio on to her favorite station. It wouldn't get static for a few hours. Her favorite singer, Adele, came on singing "Rumour Has It." How appropriate. Kelly Clarkson belted out "Stronger," followed by One Direction's "What Makes You Beautiful." She took all those songs personally and sang her heart out until the station faded away.

She put down the window, happy to have sunshine again, and breathed in the fresh air, a gift far better than any gold jewelry. The wind would tease her hair wilder than a hair stylist's touch. Cat-a-Comb stirred. She pulled up at a cheesy highway motel near Cleveland with a flashing sign saying Sleep Here, Comfortable and Clean and checked in with crate in hand. They allowed pets and it was a good thing because she wasn't staying anywhere without Cat-a-Comb.

There were so many things to take care of when they arrived in Minnesota. Stella would have to get a new doctor and have frequent mammograms to follow up on this ugly part of her life. She wished there were a doctor to make Stuart's embezzlement disappear. The bed seemed clean enough and she stretched out across it. Cat-a-Comb jumped out of his open cage and snuggled up to her, unsure of what would happen next. She needed a night's sleep and they would be on their way again.

A cobweb in the corner of the ceiling drew her eyes upward. She watched for the creative spider that had done his beautiful work. Her eyes closed. She drifted. Life with Stuart had been exciting, interesting, and full of events measuring her twenties. She would head into her thirties smarter, wiser, and more at peace. The life she had led was not a necessary life. Peace was what she craved. The designer clothes, the jewelry, the perks—

they could all disappear. Life with Stuart had been a charade. No more games.

In the morning, somewhat refreshed, they hit the road again, stopping at a convenience store for a few snacks to sustain them for a while. A few candy bars, some mints, a caffeine-laden Coke to keep her awake, some cat food, water, and a large bag of pretzels would pacify her and Cat-a-Comb and keep her steady on the road. They passed stretches of farmland, reminding her that in a short time she would arrive to walk through the fields of her own home. Cows and horses and goats and a life absolutely opposite to the one she had been living.

A bee flew into the car and startled the cat. He clawed weakly at his cage, pacing back and forth like a jungle animal. Stella would not veer off course. The bee would find its honey. Maybe she would too. Her hand brushed at the intruder until it flew out the open window. She burst into song: "Home, home on the range, where the deer and the antelope play…"

The musical notes flew away on the wings of the bee.

They would arrive in Minnesota to beautiful weather and a new and simple life.

She pushed a button and the top on the car inched upward until it shut them in. The windows closed tightly. Stella reached for a candy bar and eagerly chomped on it. Cat-a-Comb made the characteristic cry of a hungry animal and she absentmindedly flicked her fingers back toward the cage so he could lick the chocolate. "As soon as I pull over, Cat-A-Comb, I'll feed you something more nourishing." The cat meowed longingly.

It started to get dark after several hours of driving and the headlights of the oncoming cars looked like giant eyes staring back at her. Her mind wandered as she fought to stay focused on the road.

It was ironic. The source of all Steven's troubles was Stuart. He had caused trouble from the time they were small and now they were in big trouble. Steven had answered every question the police shot at him. He was a pro when it came to dealing with the cops. Now he would have to answer questions on the stand when Stuart was tried for his crimes.

At the same time he walked out of the detective's office, his triplet, Seth, headed out from a different area.

"Everything was normal in my life until I met Stuart. I thought I would get a chance to bond with the two of you, not post bond! I guess I'll see you when we testify. How stupid was I to fall into his trap?"

The cops and detectives followed them with their eyes as they walked out of the precinct.

"Let's go grab a cup of coffee and talk about the trial that will take place. All we have is the truth and the judge and jury will see how we were duped. I don't think we will be in trouble with the law. And, maybe you can lead me to the woman who is my birth mother. She has some explaining to do. I'd like to learn all that I can about my roots."

Stella breathed in the fresh country air. Cat-a-Comb bounded out of the car sniffing the grass, feeling healed after the long journey. Perhaps Stella would heal, too.

"Guess who, Mama?" Stella yelled from the front porch with Cat-a-Comb held like a football under her one arm and the screen door handle in the other.

"What? Who's there? No, it can't be. My Stella! Back from the big city after so many years!" She gave her a huge hug and patted the cat on the head. "Let me help you with your things. How long will you be here? Your papa is at day care, honey."

HEADED TO JAIL, NOT ARUBA

The sirens could be heard from all over the airport. People craned their necks to watch the police run through the airport as if they were missing their own flight. One woman whipped her neck around so hard that her pearls broke free like a runaway escaping from her mother and rolled one at a time in every direction.

Stuart was just getting up from eating his dinner. He grabbed his carry-on case by the handle and rolled it to the entrance of the restaurant just as the police stopped dead in their tracks in front of him. One of the men had a picture of him in his hands and flashed it in his face. "This is you, Stuart Crane. You are under arrest."

The party was over for Stuart. He started to shake. State prison awaited him. He would have to formally plead guilty to scheming to defraud their law firm and would probably remain locked up until he served his full punishment. His cycle of stealing from the firm and his clients to pay for his lifestyle was over. His life, as he had known it, was finished. Had he brought his brothers down with him? He had hardly gotten a chance to get to know Seth. The sweat poured down his cheeks as he was paraded through the airport like a pariah.

JUST THE BEGINNING

The house looked the same and smelled the same. There was a pie baking in the kitchen and the aroma wafted through the house. Stella wanted to run around and touch everything and tell even the inanimate objects how happy she was to have arrived safely in the warmth of her childhood home.

She would take back her old room and rule her little kingdom with her books and music and Cat-a-Comb and be happy again. She took a deep breath. Tomorrow she would take a walk on the grounds and say hello to the animals and breathe in the country air. She would find some animal buddies for Cat-a-Comb.

After much conversation with her mom and a delicious dinner unlike any gourmet restaurant could produce, she felt exhausted, kissed her mom on the forehead, and went to her bedroom that was untouched by the years. She would sleep the first peaceful slumber in months.

A NEW LIFE

The sun burst through the curtains at the crack of dawn and awoke her with a start. Stella had been used to black out shades at her homes and the brightness was overwhelming her. It made her smile. The cat let out a morning meow and they both stretched to greet the day. It was time to unpack and put things away. They would be here for some time to come and they would get very comfortable. Stella would get her dose of love from her family and heal. Maybe she would return to Philly after all of their financial affairs were settled. She was young. She could start over again. Philadelphia had been a great place to live and there were wonderful neighborhoods where a person could lead a normal life. If she missed her boutique badly enough, she could always restart her business. Stella could even move to New York to be near Cassandra when the time was right. She would make this quiet time work for her. Hard decisions would come later. Right now it was time to heal.

A quick shower and some of Mama's delicious breakfast (Oh, she could be spoiled very quickly!) and a long walk in the spring's sensual season would be the best medicine for her both physically and mentally.

Stella spoke to Cat-a-Comb just to hear her own voice.

"He's such a bastard. I have to shake him from my thoughts." She patted the cat on the head.

She grabbed a towel and headed for the bathroom hoping to wash away the anger permeating every pore.

Meow.

The goat nudged her behind and she laughed. She heard the sound come out of her mouth but almost didn't recognize it. She was enjoying herself! Stella briefly stopped to check out the cows grazing in the open meadow and walked over to the fence surrounding their property. If it needed any mending, she could do it. Momma would need all the help she could get with Papa away every day. Instead of raising livestock and crops, he was trying so hard to raise lucid thoughts in his mind. And in what seemed like a split second, her life had changed dramatically. She would rebuild. The calls had started coming in from the authorities and she would address every issue as it arose.

There was a dirt path that she had remembered riding her bike on when she was a child. It connected the neighbors' farms to theirs and was another way of staying in touch with each other.

She ran her hand along the spokes, just as she had when she took that fateful walk around her suburban neighborhood to make the biggest decision of her life that she would go home. She felt at home and she would rejuvenate here in Thief Runnery. There might not be a lot of excitement, but it would restore her health and her heart.

"Is that you, Stella?" A flatbed truck pulled up to the fence and came to a screeching halt nearly knocking down some of the posts. A handsome, blond-haired, blue-eyed, burly young man got out, shut the door and strutted over to the fence. His eyes peered through the pickets like two blue moons lit up by the sky around them. He poked his fingers through the wood posts to touch her hand.

Her fingers were on fire. "Who? Oh, my God! It's Keith, isn't it?" She put up both palms so she could feel the realness of him. "I haven't seen you since I left here more than a decade ago!" She looked into his eyes. This was the boy she had a crush on as a little girl and as a teenager. This was the boy who took her to the prom. This was the boy who waved goodbye on her last day on the farm. Her long celibacy made her loins ache. Keith had magically appeared and she could only hope he was still single. Stella remembered her mother's gossip during one of their phone conversations. She had chatted about the neighbors and their church and Stella had asked about her friend, Keith. "Why, he stayed single, Stella. He's so good to his parents," she spoke with admiration. Stella had felt a twinge of guilt that she hadn't done the same.

He could be her band-aid on this deep wound.

He was now a man. A good man. Yes, he had stayed behind to take care of his parents' place and she wanted to find out so much more.

The wind kicked up. The sun glowed and she was so happy to know that another perfect day could be expected here on their land. She had asked herself if she could return home and make it her life once again, having tasted so much more than goat's milk. *Yes,* she thought, *I have returned home.*

"Keith, I see your driving has improved! She giggled like a schoolgirl.

"Gotta have a little excitement around here. It's been dull since you left. Might think about jumping ship one of these days just like you did. Only problem is you are here and I'm not leaving!" His smile widened and his lips beckoned.

Her cell phone rang. She couldn't give up these perks. Her folks had a wall phone in the kitchen and lived in the depths of a century more Victorian than contemporary.

"Hello?" She put a finger up to indicate to Keith that she would be just a moment. She turned her back to him.

"It's Cassandra. You can't spend the rest of your life wasting away on a farm, Stella. You are too young, with your whole life ahead of you. Stay long enough to mend your heart and soul and come be with me in New York. Please think about it," she sounded as if she were begging.

All of a sudden, the cell phone felt so heavy in her hand and she yearned to turn back to Keith. "How about having dinner with us to welcome me home?" Her smile expanded across her happy face. Keith could be her temporary fix. She would repair the rest of her life in due time.

A deer bounded across the field. It reminded her of a poem she had so loved. It was from a collection entitled "Stag's Leap," written by Sharon Olds. In the poem, the speaker compared the deer emblazoned on a bottle of wine to her husband:

"When anyone escapes, my heart/leaps up. Even when it's I who am escaped from, I am half on the side of the leaver."

Even after the pained aftermath of Stuart's departure and her exodus, she would have these memories.

Would this meal with Keith be memorable, too?

"Cassandra? I'll get back to you!"

EMBEZZLEMENT: YOU ARE A PUZZLE

It is a puzzle to embezzle
To cause such trouble!
Who is this Dr. Hyde and Mr. Jekyl?
What is this warped vessel?

        Susan Hausman